Also from Robert Barnard

Last Post

✳

ROBERT BARNARD

SCRIBNER

NEW YORK   LONDON   TORONTO   SYDNEY

SCRIBNER
A Division of Simon & Schuster, Inc.
1230 Avenue of the Americas
New York, NY 10020

First Scribner hardcover edition May 2008

SCRIBNER and design are trademarks of The Gale Group, Inc.,
used under license by Simon & Schuster, Inc., the publisher of this work.

For information about special discounts for bulk purchases,
please contact Simon & Schuster Special Sales:
1-800-456-6798 or business@simonandschuster.com.

Text set in Fairfield

Manufactured in the United States of America

1   3   5   7   9   10   8   6   4   2

Library of Congress Cataloging-in-Publication Data

Barnard, Robert.
Last post / by Robert Barnard.—1st Scribner hardcover ed.
p. cm.
1. Mothers—Death—Fiction. 2. Letters—Fiction. I. Title.

PR6052.A665L37 2008
823'.914—dc22
2007037885

ISBN-13: 978-1-4767-0930-7

Last Post

CHAPTER 1

Letter to the Dead

Eve looked down at the face in the coffin. It was pretti-fied, and the neckline of the dress, the only thing visible, was too meticulously neat to suggest her mother's usual style. She wondered whether to kiss her for the last time. But she had already kissed her for the last time—as she lay dying. To kiss her now would be no kiss at all, because there was nothing remaining of her mother to receive it.

Mr. Bradshaw, the head of the firm of Bradshaw and Pollock, Funeral Directors, had not explicitly asked Eve if she wanted to see her mother laid out in her coffin. He had merely, after they had swapped funereal inanities, raised his eyebrows in the direction of the main laying-out room, and she had walked automatically, as if this was part of some ritual like exchanging rings at a wedding. Now, faced with the total extinction that was death, she felt nothing that she had not felt over and over again in the days since her mother died.

She had been with her when she died, sitting beside her in the hospital room. That was the important thing.

Eve shook herself and went back into the tactfully dim lighting of the main premises. She realized with a sinking heart that Mr. Bradshaw was preparing to be chatty.

"She'll be much missed," he said, as if he had just thought it up.

"I shall certainly miss her," Eve said, trying to be conversational, "even though we lived a fair way apart with me in Wolverhampton and her here in Crossley. We always talked to each other every week, twice a week if anything noteworthy had occurred. And we wrote quite often, particularly if it was something that was difficult to put into words."

"I remember very well when Mrs. McNabb first came to Crossley," said Mr. Bradshaw, perching himself on an empty coffin with a price tag on its lid. "I was within an ace of taking Betty, that's my eldest, out of the primary school and sending her to a private one. Then someone told me that he'd met the new teacher who was said to be going places, and who seemed enormously competent—knew what she wanted and how she wanted to achieve it. After I'd talked to your mother for a few minutes at a parents' evening, I decided to give the school a go for another year. I never regretted it, and there's a lot of parents about that time who did like me and would say the same."

"I'm so glad," said Eve, wondering when she could legitimately plead busyness and end the conversation. "I think she found being deputy rather difficult. She liked—not being in charge exactly—"

"No, no."

"—but being able to take a lead, take people along with

her. She even liked the maneuvering that convinced people they were part of the decision-making process. And she liked the compromises that had to be made, because she didn't want the reputation of being a one-woman band."

"I think it was her human side that made her such a good head. There was so often a glint in her eye."

"I think it was a Scottish sort of humor," said Eve. Then suddenly she thought: the woman we are talking about and the woman I loved and remember are two different people. And really I don't give a damn about the public woman. It's not *her* I feel like crying for. She smiled at Mr. Bradshaw.

"Well, I must get going. Always a mountain of things to do when something like this happens. The post is piling up. I am grateful to you for all you've done."

As she went out into the discreet Crossley side street, a passing man looked at her, nodded, and murmured something that was obviously a condolence or a tribute to her mother. Eve smiled her thanks and walked on—briskly, repelling any further encounters. It was time to concentrate on the private woman May McNabb.

When she got to Derwent Road, she slowed to a halt as she neared the house where she had grown up. Number 24 loomed rather pushily over the houses around and opposite it. It was an Edwardian product, with large rooms, a study and five bedrooms: it had been built for a substantial bigwig in the small town of Crossley, and it had been designed to impress. Size was of the essence and was not something to be apologized for. The garden, entirely cared for by May McNabb until an occasional

3

help had been engaged in the last months, stretched comfortably on all four sides of the house. How had her mother and father afforded this house, back in the seventies, when salaries in teaching were derisory? Maybe a legacy, maybe her father's cartoons had brought in money. Eve shook herself and walked on.

But before she could get into the home that she had shared with her mother for the first twenty years of her life, there was the neighbor in the garden. She had been there and shown signs of wanting to talk when Eve had come out earlier in the afternoon, but Eve had used her appointment with Mr. Bradshaw as an excuse, and felt that now she ought to have a few words. Mrs. Calthorp was a woman her mother had liked and respected, and she had always been good when her mother had taken a well-deserved holiday—fed the cat, collected the post, even done a bit of weeding if her mother had been away a long time. Eve stopped at her front gate. "Well, that's over," she said to the stooping form.

"Was it awful?" asked Mrs. Calthorp, straightening up.

"Not exactly. But I felt pressured to go and see the body. I suppose it's usual, and we do usual things at such a time. But I didn't want to. It was meaningless. I had seen her die."

"I know what you mean. I thought I ought to when Harold died. People even said the grandchildren ought to go, but I put a stop to *that* idea. You're quite right. It's just a charade."

"Now I want to sit down and cherish memories of her *alive*."

"I'm sure there'll be a lot of those. You were so close."

"Yes, we were. But somehow these last years, it's been difficult to *be* close. Her having school holidays and me never being able to get off then because of having to give priority to people with young children."

"Still, there were all the times you came back here, and all the weekends away."

"Those were nice, especially the weekends. Little festivals here and there. We found some good ones and some really odd ones. We'd have done much more of that sort of thing if only she'd had longer in retirement. And her keeping quiet about the breast cancer didn't help. Oh well . . ."

Eve went through her own gate and started toward the front door.

"The postman's been. Another big bundle for you," said Mrs. Calthorp, bending down.

Eve let herself into the house she had grown up in. She stepped over an untidy mess of envelopes on the doormat and went through to the kitchen. She needed so much to have a cup of tea and time for thought. The making of tea and the finding of biscuits helped, but then when she sat down in the sitting room, in her own old threadbare armchair, the thought came back to her: I only knew part of my mother—the private area. The headmistress part meant nothing to me, but it meant everything to most of those who knew her. Quite rightly she found another school for me to go to, not her own. But even the private area of her life I didn't know all that well. Visits home, phone calls, weekends at Buxton or Garsington—what did they amount to? We could have had such a good time now that she had reached sixty-five. Gone around together, made discoveries about each other. The process was beginning in the six months after she retired. And then the beastly cancer intervened—suddenly, and quickly deadly.

She fetched the post and began to open the envelopes. Mostly short missives about how sad people were, how much her mother had meant to them, how wonderfully she had turned around the Blackfield Road Primary School. All of the messages heartfelt, this Eve felt sure of. There were hardly any purely formal condolences. The longer ones usually mentioned one or two special memories of her mother—as teacher, headmistress or just as a sympathetic and enterprising human being. Eve had to admit that many of the anecdotes caught the essence of her mother in her public role.

She was nearing the end of her task, with two piles on the floor beside her: those needing answers and those that did not. She picked up an envelope that had been near the bottom of the raggedy pile she had taken up from the doormat. It was fatter than the earlier ones, with a fierce animal on a first-class stamp and, as usual these days, an illegible postmark. She opened it and found four small pages of very flimsy paper covered with large, clear script. When she read the inscription she realized with a shock that the writer was not one of those who wanted to pay tribute to a dead woman.

Dearest May,

It seems ages since we've been in touch, and I can only explain the scrappiness of my letters by pleading the extreme busyness of someone who has madly taken up this and that these last few years, and has less time than she ever had in her life before. Don't do anything as silly now that you have retired!

My activities are easily cataloged, though they take up so much of my time. Apart from all my church work, which I've told you about before, I am a school governor, I am secretary to the local Green Party and I dabble as often as I am asked and can manage it in amateur dramatics. People say that there are few parts for older women, but I think they must mean few *good* parts, few long, meaty ones. I am now into my third production of *Hay Fever*. In the first I played Myra, in the second I played Judith Bliss, and now I'm going to play Clara the old maid. Plenty of meat in that part if you know how to dig for it. But how amateur dramatics do bring home to one the passing of time!

But sometimes, you know, it's as if time has not passed at all, and we are back, together again and happy as sand boys. Often at night I dream of you being beside me in bed, with your lovely enticing body throwing out invitations even in sleep. We were the most wonderful pair, May; two people who had to come together because physically and men-tally, we made a complete whole, and were quite diminished by separation. Oh dear—I did so love you, May darling, and I sometimes feel bitter that you did not have the courage to make the sort of stand that women of our tastes make all the time nowadays. And when I'm in that mood, I feel it wasn't the business with John that separated us, but your own conventionality and lack of fighting spirit.

Oh well—water under the bridge. You'll wish I hadn't mentioned it, I know. But how wonderful it was. I feel invigorated just by the memory of it. Have fun in your retirement, dearest.

With all my love,
Jean

Eve sat in silence with the letter in her hand as outside the sun went down and evening came on.

CHAPTER 2

Back from the Dead

"Grant?"

The uncertainty in her voice had never been more audible.

"Eve! Hi! Why do you sound as if you wish you were talking to someone else?"

"That's not how I sound. But we did say we'd keep in touch as old friends who'd also been something more."

"So?"

"This is . . . well, rather more than 'old friends' stuff. Grant, my mother has died."

"Oh, I am sorry. We didn't meet all that often, but I really liked her. And respected her as well. How come? Was it some kind of accident?"

"Breast cancer. It killed her quite quickly, though she kept quiet about it longer than I like. But I was able to be with her when she died."

"That will be a comfort. But are you having problems coming to terms with it?"

"No, it's not that. Or not exactly. And everyone in

Crossley has been marvelous—telling me how much she meant to them, what a difference she made to their lives. And there's been a veritable deluge of letters, most of them just a bit personal, which has been nice. She would have been tickled pink . . ."

"But?"

"I got back from the funeral parlor this afternoon. There was another pile of letters and cards. One of them from someone—I don't know the name or handwriting, no reason why I should. Grant, could I e-mail it to you? I'd like to know what you think."

"I'm flattered. Is it as a psychiatrist you're consulting me?"

"No, as an old friend with his feet usually on the ground. Would you ring me back when you've read it through and thought about it for a while? Really do *think*, Grant. I've done nothing but that since I read it. The number to ring is the old one: 0136 724163. I'll be in all evening."

She herself had done all the thinking she could manage. She had first grasped at the straw that the writer was a Frenchman—Jean. She had grabbed the letter, and the reference to *Hay Fever* had jumped out at her, and then the handwriting: this was the sort of script instilled into one at a good girls' school, not that of any French man or woman.

Then she had wondered if it was some kind of cruel joke. Many grown-up people nourished grievances against their teachers. News of her mother's death could have aroused some such old grudge . . . Except that the old grudge should surely have been against *herself*, to take such a form. She, not her mother, was the one whom the letter had hurt and bewildered. And who, in or around Crossley, where the news of the death would have spread, could have a grudge against Eve? She had left the place eighteen years before with, so far as she knew, a quite spotless reputation.

Now, having typed and e-mailed the letter, she let her thoughts stray on another path. Why did she mind so much? She had nothing against lesbians. She had known plenty, liked some, disliked others, as with any other group of people. Why should she mind if at some point in her life her mother had had an affair with someone of her own sex?

Eve had had enough experience—especially during the Grant years—of looking into herself and analyzing her feelings to come up with the answer quite quickly: she resented not knowing about this side of her mother, finding out about it in this way. Even before she had opened the letter she had been feeling guilt about not being closer to her mother in her adult years. Now the guilt was assuaged by this easy way of blaming her mother. But if they had had more time together as adults, her mother would surely have filled her in on her relations with this person called Jean, on this aspect of her life. Wouldn't she?

But thinking about it, that argument didn't seem watertight. During their weekends at arts festivals they had often enough seen or met up with obvious lesbian couples. Why had May not taken the opportunity to share her past with her daughter? If Eve had been a negligent daughter, it would seem that May had been a negligent mother.

Then another thought struck her. Her mother had hardly ever talked about her husband, Eve's father. Why not? And why had Eve herself shown so little curiosity about him?

This was followed swiftly by another thought. What exactly did the letter say about her father? She took up the flimsy page again. "The business with John that separated us." What exactly did that mean? An *affaire trois* which had been won by the heterosexual partner?

Considering it in the cold light of evening, the statement even began to sound slightly sinister.

She was glad when the telephone rang. For all his shortcomings—and pomposity was the main one, the one that had killed their relationship—Grant was a comforting presence at times of crisis.

"That was a stunner," his rich, calm voice said.

"Yes, it was."

"And your first thought was: I should have known."

"Yes, it was. You know me so well. Not put into words, but . . . Why on earth didn't she tell me? Just an off-the-cuff remark. 'I tried it once, but it wasn't for me'—that sort of thing."

"Perhaps she looked back on it with distaste, even shame."

"My mother was never one for shame—not for wallowing in it, anyway. Pick up your luggage, learn from your mistake and pass on—that was more her line."

"But if she was pressured into it—the sex—and found it unpleasant?"

"Pressured? My mother? Anyway, I didn't get the impression from the letter that anything like that happened. It was more that she was pressured away from her natural bent."

"Well, that may be your interpretation, but it wouldn't be how Jean viewed it, would it? If the affair was one of the emotional high spots of her life? She wouldn't want to acknowledge that your mother had had to be pressured."

"It's so difficult at this distance of time. And Mother never having touched on the subject so far as I can remember."

There was silence at the other end.

"Eve, I'm not sure this is getting us anywhere."

"No, it's not. But what should I *do*, Grant?"

"You know what I think of your questions like that."

"That they're preparatory to my doing exactly what I've already decided to do."

"Precisely!"

"But in this case I haven't decided anything. I just don't know what to do."

"Maybe. Still, I don't think you'll like what I would recommend. That is that you do precisely nothing."

"I thought it would be that."

"After all, why should you do anything? Your dead mother had a lesbian affair in the past. So what? She never told you. Tough, but that was her decision, one she had a right to make. So why can't you just move on?"

Eve thought.

"But what about the reference to my father?"

"Was that John? I don't think I ever heard his name. You didn't talk about him."

"Yes, his name was John McNabb. I never knew him. Mother didn't talk about him."

"You never asked her?"

"I expect I did. But not very urgently, obviously. You blame me for that, don't you?"

"You know psychiatrists don't much go in for blame. But it does surprise me."

"Mother was obviously all I wanted, and I didn't need to imagine a benevolent, wise, lost father."

Eve was silent for a moment before asking her next question.

"Did you get the feeling that the pair of them, Jean and May, had done or tried to do something serious, something perhaps to stymie John and his claims on my mother?"

"To tell you the truth, I didn't think much at all about that sentence. Probably I would have if I'd known your father's name . . . Yes, maybe you're right. What *do* you know about your father? All you've told me is that he is dead."

"Yes—he died when I was about three or four."

"Any memories of him in the house?"

"Hardly anything, and I don't remember anything that was there earlier on but is now gone. That I do find odd. Mother was not sentimental, but she wasn't ruthless either. Clearing him away like that seems out of character."

"You actually remember asking her about him?"

"Yes, occasionally. Once I remember asking about him and I was shown a photograph. That obviously satisfied me at the time. Maybe her coldness on the subject was her way of shutting me up."

"Seems to me there must be things of his, or things

about him, in the house. Some wives in unhappy marriages have a spring clean of everything that reminds them of their dead husband. Did you ever get the impression that your father was hated?"

"No, certainly not. But then, I never got any impression of him at all."

"She could just have put any things of his away somewhere—the attic, a high cupboard—that sort of thing. Worth trying."

"Yes. I've thought of doing that."

"Don't you even know what he did for a living?" There was an edge of exasperation in his voice. Exasperation was his substitute for blame. He thought her lack of curiosity was blameworthy.

"Oh yes, I know that. He was a cartoonist."

There was a moment's silence.

"Well, that's more interesting than a train driver or a bank clerk, isn't it? Who did he cartoon for?"

"Oh, I think it was *The Scotsman*. Or maybe the *Glasgow Herald* or *Tribune* or something."

"Right. Were these daily political cartoons?"

Eve really had to think.

"No, I think they were human interest cartoons. Gentle." Her voice brightened. "That's right. Mother said they were gentle and she went on: 'He was a gentle man.' I remember now. There was a central family in the cartoons, and it was the funny things they did or said, and their comic dog and cat—that kind of thing. Sort of like the Gambols in the *Express*."

"Oh," said Grant, who was a taste snob: anything that had gone out of fashion was deplorable in his eyes. "Well, let's hope that he was funnier. Do you realize you've just endowed your father with his first characteristic, his first human trait?"

"Yes, I suppose I have."

"If these two determined women ganged up on him, he probably didn't stand a chance."

Eve smiled to herself.

"I suspect you have just tried very hard to avoid using the word 'dykes,' and not to suggest they must have been sergeant-major types in drag." Grant laughed. He was usually honest about his prejudices with Eve. "Anyway, you're ignoring one thing."

"What's that?"

"The fact that, as far as we know, my father won and the lesbian experiment failed. Does 'Jean' sound like someone who enjoyed a great triumph all those years ago?"

"No," admitted Grant. "She sounds like someone who suffered defeat, and has never been able to put it behind her."

"Agreed. So granted I'm going to do something, what do I do?"

Grant pondered.

"No address on the letter. Presumably she didn't put an address on the envelope, as the Americans do?"

"No."

"What about the postmark?"

"Terribly smudged, as they usually are these days. I think the post office doesn't want us to know when things were posted."

"You could consult a philatelist. Postmarks are probably important to them. He might be able to give you an idea of the length of the town name it was posted from, maybe even the initial letter."

"Maybe. That doesn't get us awfully far though, does it?"

"No. But you've got a two-pronged approach now. Your mother's possible lesbian affair, and the 'business with John' that Jean talks about. Plenty on your plate for a start. Do you know, for example, when your mother took the school job in Crossley?"

"Oh—when I was very young. No—before I was born, because I was born here. I never remember living anywhere else until I was grown up."

"Pin it down. And where did she come from?"

"Melrose, in the Border country. She always said she took care to minimize her Scottish accent and vocabulary when first she came here. She thought the first priority was to be understood by the children."

"Unfashionable but sensible," said Grant. "And was your father still alive then? And if so, did he come with her?"

Silence from Eve for some time.

"I really don't know. My mother was here for such a long time that it seems like she was always here. But my father—I just didn't ask about the details, so I don't know."

"Well, you'll pay for your lack of curiosity by having a mountain to climb. Still, there must be plenty of people in Crossley who remember when your mother arrived there. Get on to them, and see what they know—about your father and any other friends of your mother. Good luck. But remember I recommended you to do nothing at all."

And would always be quick to remind her of that if

things went wrong, thought Eve. Her immediate reaction to the conversation was satisfaction that she had Grant as a friend, and even greater satisfaction that she no longer had him as a romantic partner. As long as something so ingrained, so much part of him, as his sleek self-satisfaction grated on her, there was no prospect of a really loving long-term relationship. She had always enjoyed her mother's descriptions, out of Grant's hearing, of psychology as "pseudo-science" and "high-class mumbo jumbo," and she wouldn't have done if she had real respect for his profession. No, that part of her life was over, and well over, and Grant would never again be more than a valued friend.

Later that evening Eve poured herself a drink from one of the bottles her mother had left—bottles that had probably all been bought at Christmas and had lasted from Christmas to Christmas. Unless in those last weeks May had turned to alcohol as a deadener of pain and fear. With a stiff brandy in her hand Eve went from room to room, looking into drawers and cupboards, noting a few things that had been moved since she had lived there, and the many that were just where she remembered them. All the cupboards too contained just what she remembered— quite naturally: the top of the hall cupboard was piled rather untidily with scarves, gloves and woolly hats, just as she would have expected. There was a kitchen cupboard full of glasses and pudding plates and unwanted mugs, just as it had been when she was a young girl.

But she did see that high up there were tops of cupboards which contained she knew not what. She rejected the idea of fetching a ladder or the library steps and having a look there and then. Much better to do it in daylight, and without having taken a drop.

In the bathroom she looked up and saw the covered-over hole that was the access to the attic. She never remembered having been up there. For all she knew it could be empty. But she was beginning to hope not.

Next morning she ran out of eggs with her breakfast, so the first thing she did was to walk into town and do a shop for the everyday necessities. Then, hoping he began the day early, she went down the side street that led to Bradshaw and Pollock and was delighted to find Mr. Bradshaw in and improving the shining hour. She dealt with some more details of the burial, then, feeling the abruptness of it, she turned the conversation round to one of her current preoccupations.

"Thinking ahead to the gravestone," she said, "I suppose it's usual to put 'wife of' or some such formula."

"That's entirely a matter of choice," said Bradshaw.

"It's so long ago, isn't it?" said Eve. "Thinking about it, I wish I had pressed my mother more on the subject of my father. But I never had any memories of him. I know almost nothing beyond the fact that his name was John McNabb and he was a newspaper cartoonist. Did he come down with my mother when she took the job in Crossley?"

"Oh yes. I met him—to say hello to—more than once."

"What were your impressions of him?"

"A very nice man: quiet, effacing, just the right sort for your mother we all thought."

"Why that? Why did she need an effacing husband?"

Mr. Bradshaw considered.

"You know, in this job one sees an awful lot of marriages, with an enormous variety of combinations, successful and unsuccessful. One I've come to recognize—and as often as not it's a successful combination—is the determined, ambitious, strong-minded woman married to a quiet, supportive man who enjoys being in the background. I suppose it's a direct reversal of the Victorian pattern, but it works very well sometimes. It's the Mrs. Thatcher and Dennis pattern, isn't it?"

"Oh dear," said Eve. "I don't think my mother would like that comparison. She called Maggie Thatcher 'the milk snatcher' to the end of her days."

"She probably wouldn't like the words 'ambitious' and 'strong-minded' for herself, but she was both."

"But she stayed here for thirty-odd years."

"When you're head of a good primary school, there's nowhere else to go except into administration or politics. I suspect that neither prospect attracted your mother."

"Definitely not. So you met my father—where?"

"Oh, a couple of parents' evenings, I think. He came along to fetch May at the end, with the baby—you."

"Yes, me. Do you have any other memories?"

"Not really. Gentle, persuasive, quietly humorous. I'm not being very helpful, am I? But it's a long time ago."

"I'm very grateful to you. And you've told me at least one thing I didn't know: that my father came down with my mother to Crossley."

And she had also learned that Mr. Bradshaw, though probably close to his seventies, had an excellent memory for small matters. Perhaps in his profession it was helpful never to forget a face.

When she reached home she felt as though she was riding on the beginnings of a wave. And the name of that wave was John McNabb. She wandered around the downstairs rooms, identifying places where things might be put away and then forgotten. Her father had died when she was a small girl and it was perhaps most likely that at some point anything that had been kept that referred to him would either have been thrown out or transferred to the attic. Still, at some stage she was going to have a clear out, so it was natural to start now. She got a stepladder from the garden shed, then the biggest cardboard box that she could find. She climbed up to the highest cupboard in a seventies-style set of units, where the television and the CD player sat, along with open spaces for china and glass and big cupboards for games and toys at the bottom. The top cupboard was very high, and from the moment she opened it she realized that its contents were miscellaneous. She brought down stage by stage piles of newspapers and cuttings, odd prints in simple frames, a box of letters and forms, none of them personal, then a pile of old books that had outlived their usefulness—old Companion Book Club volumes, Jilly Cooper novels, a children's encyclopedia and at the back an old, shiny but cracked photograph album.

She climbed down carefully, cradling it to her breast, and took it to her old chair in the sitting room. It was only half used—her mother had never been much use at photography, or had much time for people who took photos instead of concentrating on the experience itself. A picture of May, her sister and their parents on the front porch of their house in Melrose began the book. The hostility to photography was mirrored in May's face. Her grandparents Eve did remember, particularly her grand-dad, who had died when she was eighteen. May had never been close to her sister, who had died a couple of years ago. There were one or two other childhood photos, and then one with a male friend probably from teachers' college. That would be about 1960 or so. No sign of miniskirts yet, and probably they wouldn't have been allowed in college.

Then at last one of John McNabb, cradling her in the garden at the back of the house in which she now sat. His face was shadowed as he looked down at his baby daughter. She turned the page.

Here it was at last, a genuine likeness. It was a black-and-white studio portrait, perhaps made for professional purposes. Maybe his newspaper printed the portrait with one of his cartoons from time to time. He looked out shyly from under a lock of hair, his mouth turned traditionally upward in a tiny smile, perhaps requested by the photographer. Nice, humorous, unremarkable. Was Mr. Bradshaw wrong? Did John McNabb turn out to be quite the wrong husband for the determined woman who had called herself to the end May McNabb?

CHAPTER 3

Bakemeats

It was a long time since Eve had been to a funeral. The last one must have been—oh, poor Bella Porter, who committed suicide after she had been diagnosed as having womb cancer. Memory stirred great pity in her: Bella had always said she was an awful coward where pain was concerned, and pills and more pills had seemed to her an unpleasant lesser of two evils. Cancer . . . So often cancer these days. She looked down at her feet as a substitute for praying.

She had been led to the front pews of dear old St. John the Evangelist, and she had been overwhelmed by nostalgia as the much-loved building cast its spell. It had figured prominently not in family occasions but in school and communal events during the nineteen years of her residence in Crossley. Now she rather wished she had insisted on being seated at the back. Quite apart from the fact that she could have seen the whole nave and the altar better, she would also have had the backs of people's heads to recognize them by. Ensconced in the pews for family at the front she had nothing but the occasional raised voice to guess who were taking their places behind her. She had a definite sense that the church was filling up. She couldn't look around for fear she would be judged as assessing the turnout. Or even condemning the absentees. In fact it was a wonderful turnout, considering they must all be friends, colleagues, former pupils, even mere casual acquaintances. There was no family left, apart from her. And she no longer even had a partner to swell the number to two.

"That place is vacant, isn't it? I'll just squeeze past."

The voice came from the aisle, a couple of rows back. Eve knew it at once, or knew that she had known it, but now couldn't place it. She had to restrain herself from peering around at the newcomer. It was a couple of minutes to eleven o'clock. The vicar had stressed that everything should be done to time, since the church was booked for a wedding in the afternoon and would need to be decorated. Eve felt satisfaction in this continuing chain of the vital milestones of most people's lives. Perhaps she could look around when the coffin began its journey up the aisle. The voice was so individual: a cracked, assertive voice, one that assumed its right to bear witness, its duty to voice its opinions, however cranky and ill-informed they might be. A voice unheard since her childhood days, and only once then.

Aunt Ada.

But surely it couldn't be Aunt Ada. Not that she was necessarily dead. She was only eight or nine years older than May, and in fact a cousin rather than an aunt. But the breach between the two women had been total, and

Aunt Ada surely would not want to attend the funeral. Her mother had not mentioned her for years—probably not since she, Eve, was in her teens. She had seen (and *heard*) her once, at a family funeral, and had been fascinated. Apart from that, Eve had never met her and knew of her mainly through her mother's hostility. Oh God—if it was Ada she would have to be asked to the funeral bakemeats afterward. Her pushing her way into the front pews suggested she was going to assert her status as "family."

The coffin began its journey to the front of the church, and everyone stood. Then the vicar took charge, an unusually precise yet commanding figure. They prayed, they sang "Guide Me, Oh Thou Great Jehovah," then George Wilson, May's deputy at Blackfield Road Primary for many years, read a poem. Eve had wavered between "No Coward Soul" and a Sylvia Plath, but she thought the Emily Brontë too metaphysical for her mother's down-to-earth tastes and habits, and she then remembered May's disapproval of a mother whose suicide appeared to her a dereliction of duty. She definitely would not have wanted Sylvia Plath. Finally Eve had decided—this was before the arrival of The Letter—that there was no earthly reason why the poem should be by a woman, and she had chosen "When the Present Has Latched Its Postern Behind My Tremulous Stay," and Hardy's view of the afterlife still seemed to her not unlike May's, though her life had been very much more than a tremulous stay. The reading, very well prepared, as May would have expected, cheered her up, and she listened with good grace to the vicar's not entirely accurate rehearsal of the facts she had given him about May's life. There was no mention of a husband, but then she had not mentioned him to the vicar. Next there was a lesson, they sang "Love Divine, All Love Excelling" and via the vicar Eve invited all friends of her mother to refreshments (she couldn't think of anything else to call them), and then slowly the coffin was taken out into the churchyard and toward the dug grave. Eve followed slowly after it.

Now she was out in the open air she could assess the congregation. There were all the teachers at Blackfield Road Primary, and many older ones now retired. There were teachers from the local comprehensive, and above all there were ordinary Crossley people from all walks and classes of life, people who wanted to pay tribute to a local institution, someone who they felt had been a good influence on their lives. Eve was marking down people it might be interesting to talk to and went through the ceremonies at the graveside in a dream, vaguely wondering what the scattering of earth was meant to symbolize.

Suddenly she was seized upon by a trio of women, one of them her mother's age, the other two probably in their forties.

"We just wanted to say," said the senior of them, "how sad your mother's death made us, and how much we owed her."

"We went to school *under* your mother," said one of the middle-aged ones, "that's the only way I can put it, and then our sons and daughter did, and in a couple of years' time two grandchildren will start at the same school."

"I cried when I thought my grandchildren would not

have the experience," said the other woman. "But then your mother retired, so they would have missed her anyway. *Such* a shame she didn't have a long retirement."

"I've been thinking the same," said Eve. "We had planned to do so many things together."

"She might even have married again," said the oldest of them. "But of course she could have done that earlier if she'd wanted to."

"She was so busy," said Eve, almost apologetically. "She never had time, it seems. Did you know my father?"

"Oh no. I was newly married when your mother and father came here, and had no children. The only thing I've heard was that he was likable. Very approachable, people said."

"Well, that's nice to hear."

"But did your mother never—?"

"She didn't talk about him much. I suppose she must have found the subject painful."

Then she turned, seized the arm of George Wilson to thank him for his reading of the Hardy and started with him toward the church hall.

When they got there and went inside, she whispered to George, "I'd like to talk to you later—you will stay, won't you?" and when he nodded she went around to press flesh, welcome and thank people, invite them to eat the sandwiches and fruitcake and drink the tea, coffee or white wine the catering firm had provided. She was met with enormous friendliness, tales of gratitude to her mother for this or that, and assurances that she would not soon be forgotten in the community.

Would a small, old-fashioned community like Crossley be as wholehearted in its enthusiasm if they had known that May had had a lesbian relationship in her past? Eve had to admit that she didn't know the answer to that question. Times had changed—but how much had they changed in Crossley?

While she was engaged on her last duty as a daughter, she was aware of the figure of Aunt Ada, gaunt and unprepossessing, lurking in the background, occasionally talking to people similarly alone, but mostly standing by the food table and tucking in almost nonstop. It occurred to Eve that she could be one of those pensioners who went to any funeral that might offer free food. When the sound of Ada's voice did reach her ears, it invariably had the same old croak of disapproval, or sneer or open self-congratulation. At one point she thought she heard the dreaded words, "I'm not like that. I say what I think."

When she had been shaking hands, thanking and encouraging all to eat and drink for over half an hour, she thought the time had come when she could put off no longer the encounter with the only other family member present. She walked over to the lank, scrawny figure, a smile on her face and her hand outstretched.

"I think you must be my aunt Ada."

The cadaverous face glanced at the hand, then resumed piling her plate with prawn sandwiches. Eve thought of keeping the hand outstretched until she was shamed into taking it, but she thought Ada was unaware of the emotion of shame, so she tucked it away.

"Did you think the service was appropriate?"

A sneer blossomed on her face.

"I suppose he earned his fee. He did what he was called on to do: said all the things people wanted to hear, and none of the things that they didn't want to."

"I suppose they generally do, don't they? . . . Did you and she make it up in her last years?"

"Make it up?" Her face creased up questioningly, and looked like a deflated rugby ball. "I don't know what you mean. We never talked, if that's what you were asking. No call to."

"I wondered why you came to the funeral."

"I saw the notice in the *Yorkshire Evening Post*. It's family, isn't it? Hardly any of us left. I thought I might as well come along."

"You're very welcome. And it means I'm not completely on my own. It's sad you never phoned Mother and made things up—you living so close."

"What's that got to do with it? Didn't change things. She didn't want to have anything to do with me, and I certainly didn't want to have anything to do with her."

"It must have been something serious that brought about the split."

"You could say that."

"Will you tell me what it was?"

Aunt Ada leaned the top half of her body forward in confidential mode, then decided to prolong her period in the limelight. She drew back.

"You wouldn't want to know. It's a long time ago."

"It is. And I *would* want to know what brought about such a long estrangement."

"Estrangement? I don't know about that. We were never close."

"But other than me, you were the last family she had, after her father and sister died. Please, I think I have a right to be told what the cause was."

Aunt Ada leaned forward again.

"There were rumors going around. In the family, or what was left of it. In Melrose too. Her father heard them, and he blustered away—said they were tittle-tattle and there was nothing in them. Then I saw them together in Manchester. Walking together down Dean Street, laughing and *holding hands*."

It was as much as Eve could do not to burst out laughing.

"A lot of women hold hands. A lot more women have pleasure in each other's company without being lesbians."

"Not those two. And I didn't mention a woman, so you've obviously heard. Didn't shock you, I suppose. Young people don't shock, more's the pity. Anyway I followed them to the Gallery Hotel (not somewhere I could afford for myself) and they went in for lunch. They had a table by the window, and I could watch them from the other side of the road. They were like lovers: looking into each other's eyes, giggling at each other's jokes, hands on knees, hands on hands—you name it, one of their hands had been there . . . I said to myself when I decided to come here that I wouldn't tell you this."

"Did you really? You were still thinking about it, after all this time?"

"You forced it out of me, so you've only yourself to blame. So now you know: that's why me and May never spoke in the last years of her life."

"More than thirty years, that must have been."

"That's right. I have my principles, me. I never go soft."

"That must be a great comfort. Eat up. If the prawn sandwiches have run out, there are still plenty of egg-and-cress ones. You won't go hungry."

And conscious that she was repressing with difficulty the impulse to order Aunt Ada out of the reception— repressing it for the sole reason that it was she who had prompted the expression of Ada's antediluvian prej-udices—Eve retreated to the far corner of the now-emptying church hall to the more comfortable and comforting figure of George Wilson.

He must now be, she reckoned, in his early seventies— older than her mother, whose loyal deputy he had been for many years, turning Blackfield Road Primary into a local beacon for stability, with his genuine love of children and the value he placed on learning. Probably the school, with its new head, was now finding that stability came at a price and that in many areas it was time for change. May would have understood that. But she had valued George Wilson's unfailing support—always stretching to warnings of possible trouble—which most people would have expected from the persona he presented to the world: plump of figure, firm of step, with a twinkling eye and an untidy mustache. Eve had always loved him, and remembered playing with him in the garden when she was on her first tricycle. Presumably her father's early death had prevented her having any similar memories of him.

"Problem?" he asked, looking at her with understanding.

"You could say that."

"One of the rellies, as Australians say?"

"Yes. Or rather the only one. Which makes it rather sad."

"She *looks* a problem, but what's her beef?"

"She hadn't spoken to Mother for thirty years or so, and she came to the funeral to scoff half the food and to spread—reluctantly, of course, so why the relish in her eyes?—stories about my mother that she is now in no position to rebut."

"Hmmm. I wouldn't worry too much about that," said George in his well-known calming-the-whirlwind voice. "I can't think of anyone who was less likely than your mother to be the subject of gossip or calumny. A life lived beyond reproach, that's how I see her. And *that* woman—somehow just the look of her, and certainly the hearing of her voice, makes one uneasy. Sometimes one automatically distrusts what someone says because of the way they say it. I stood near her for half a minute, and I wouldn't trust her an inch."

"I think you're bang on target there," said Eve with a feeling of relief. "But the nasty old bat was talking about rumors—rumors that had even reached my mother's hometown, Melrose."

"Well, they kept up the Scottish connection, you know. Through your father's job on the *Glasgow Tribune,* and your mother's family."

"So it was the *Tribune?* I wasn't sure. George, you were here when my mother and my father moved down from Scotland, weren't you?"

"Yes, I was. I was a wet-behind-the-ears young teacher, though I was two years older than she was."

"What were your impressions of them?"

"A lovely young woman, first-rate at her job, and John a talented artist. Ideal combination. She was very young when she got the deputy headship a year or so later, but she had had a brilliant record at teachers' college, and two teaching positions that she filled outstandingly well—everyone agreed about that."

"How did she fit in here?"

"Beautifully. She was such an inspiring teacher, everyone liked her and she transformed the organization of the school."

"Was that popular with the actual head?"

George Wilson hesitated.

"I wasn't going to say anything about that. There were a few problems as the years went by—not at first, so far as I know. But Evelyn Southwell was a difficult woman, not by nature a leader figure or an organizer, so May found herself doing more and more of the head's jobs as time went by. The fact that Evelyn gave her the jobs to do didn't make her less prickly if she thought her authority was being bypassed or questioned. That's human nature, I suppose."

"I see. And then when she retired, Mother got the job?"

"She didn't retire, she moved on. But yes . . . Yes, there was no question your mother deserved it."

"You haven't said much about my father. I should say I have no memories of him, and hardly any memory of really talking about him with my mother."

George Wilson thought, but his response was disappointing.

"I certainly saw him now and then, had chats with him. He seemed a nice chap."

"Did he come down to live with my mother?"

George had to think.

"Yes. They had a council house briefly, while they were looking around. Then they bought the house that I imagine you've just inherited."

"How did they afford it—young, and not long married?"

"He was a cartoonist with a fairly important newspaper. It doesn't qualify down here as a national newspaper, but it certainly does in Scotland. And housing was much cheaper then—more affordable in relation to normal incomes."

"Yes, of course. You hesitated a bit when I asked if John came down to live here . . ."

"Only because he had to go up to Scotland for, I think, a couple of days a week. Wednesdays and Thursdays, I seem to remember. They had to get someone to look after you those days. It was Elsie Brinsley, wife of one of the older teachers in the school. A motherly type, I recall. I suppose the paper insisted he be around part of the week."

Eve thought.

"Or he could have been two-timing my mother."

"Is that what the old bat over there suggested?" Wilson asked. He looked over in Aunt Ada's direction. "My God— those sandwiches disappear, don't they?"

"It doesn't matter. Most people have gone. She'll go on to what's left of the cakes, I expect . . . No, as a matter of fact that wasn't what she suggested. I'd rather not talk about that."

"And by the sound of it, she shouldn't have brought it up at the funeral of the person concerned."

"She shouldn't, but I'm partly to blame. And she speaks her mind, as she'll tell you. With that sort of mind, it would be much better if she didn't."

"Okay then, I won't press you any further."

"Let's just say I had a letter the other day that upset me."

"Provenance?"

"An unknown woman. Thought mother was still alive. No address, postmark illegible."

"Well, as I say, I won't pry. But I do know a chap who's a whiz-kid philatelist. Used to be a pupil at Blackfield Road. He's a policeman now by day, and runs a philatelic business by night or when he's off duty. I'll give you his address. Can't do any harm."

"That could be useful. Though by the way, I won't have any use for the policeman side. What worries me is not connected with crime."

"I never thought it was. I was just filling you in . . . But you know, Eve, if this is a private, personal matter, and if it was something your mother kept from you—"

Eve sighed.

"I know, I know. Is this the time to break down her silence?"

"No. Is *any* time right to do that? You have no duty to ferret out her secrets."

"No. But there is a side issue, and that seems to concern my father. He's not around to fight his corner. I would like to get to the bottom of it. To tell you the truth, I feel quite guilty that I made almost no effort while Mother was alive to find out anything at all about my father. Why didn't I? I just can't explain why not. And certainly Mother never rushed in to tell me. And now I feel a niggling curiosity about him, just when it has become impossible to get any information from her."

Eve was conscious of George's deep, dependable gaze being fixed on her. She was conscious too that she had not been telling him the whole truth. She was, if necessary, going to invade her mother's posthumous privacy.

"I'll write down the chappie's address for you," said George. "He's Indian, from a Hindu family. I apologize if the spelling is a bit haywire."

The moment had passed, and Eve was glad it had.

She looked around. Aunt Ada had consumed her last egg-and-cress sandwich and had her last slice of fruitcake and was departing alone through the door. Eve bade her no farewells. She felt suddenly hungry herself and went and sampled the cake, the apple sponge and one last sandwich, a corned beef one, just beginning to turn up at the edges. Soon she was the last person in the room, and there was no excuse for not going home.

Eve was not happy with herself. That warning from George Wilson had been a reproach, and she felt the need to justify herself to herself, and yet couldn't. She did want to find out the truth about her mother. Had May lived a lie throughout her adult life? If so, she, Eve, did not blame her. The blame should be attached to the times May had lived in, to the people who cherished old prejudices, to the popular press, so strident and vicious in Great Britain.

And blame was, in truth, no part of Eve's plan. She wanted to find out the truth about her mother simply because she wanted to *know*. And she wanted to know because she thought she should have been told.

She suddenly realized she did not want to go back to her job. She never wanted to see Wolverhampton again. She never wanted to persuade herself that the Midlands countryside was quite as beautiful as West Yorkshire. She wanted to stay in Yorkshire, where she had grown up.

It occurred to her that she had left here to be independent, to have her own secrets, to get away from a much-loved mother who expected to know everything about what her daughter was doing. Now the positions were reversed, and she was trying to find out what her mother had got up to all those years ago around the time of Eve's birth.

CHAPTER 4

Postmark

Eve had no weapons to combat the emptiness of an evening at home after a funeral. She would have liked to go to a pub and sit alone with her thoughts over a couple of drinks, but there was no pub in the vicinity of Crossley where she was not likely to encounter somebody who had memories of Blackfield Road and its headmistresses, and she had no stomach for a long drive. In the end she put jacket potatoes in the oven, then made a meal that could be cooked from frozen, and ate alone with a glass of wine. Alone. It seemed to strike the keynote of her life at the moment. Well, alone was better than being with Aunt Ada. But not better than being with Grant, that she had to admit. With all his pomposity and dogmatism, he could be entertaining and was almost always stimulating. She put the thought from her: that was a part of her past. She sighed aloud. She had only old, failed relationships to meditate on, not the prospect of future ones.

Faced with the yawning waste of the rest of the evening, with nothing but cheap trivia on television and cheap chat on radio, she fished in her handbag and brought out the slip of paper given her by George Wilson. The name of the stamp expert was Omkar Rani, and he lived at 23 Butterfield Road, Bradford. His phone number was 01274 867210. What had she to lose?

The voice that replied to her ring was female, and not speaking English.

"Could I speak to Omkar Rani please?"

"He not in."

"Could you tell me when he will be in?"

"He home eight o'clock."

"Thank you. I'll phone sometime after that."

When she did phone, at half past, the voice that answered was sharper and brighter, and hardly at all accented.

"Omkar Rani speaking."

"Oh, hello. Er . . . I rang you earlier—"

"Yes. My wife told me."

"It's rather difficult. I'd better say at once it's not a police matter. It is a philatelic one."

"Good. I almost never get rung on police matters at home, but it's pleasant that it's a philatelic call. What are you interested in?"

Eve quickly put her thoughts in order.

"I perhaps should explain from the start that I'm not in the least interested in stamps. I believe you went to Blackfield Road school. You probably remember my mother, who died ten days ago. May McNabb."

"Oh, Mrs. McNabb. I remember her so well, and I was so sad about her dying. Sixty-seven is no age these days. And I have so many happy memories from that school."

"I'm glad. Many people have told me that. The fact is, I received a letter a few days ago—it was a letter to my mother from someone who had not heard of her death. I don't want to go into what upset me, but I would like to know the area it comes from. There is no address on the letter or on the envelope, no surname either in the signature. There is only the postmark."

"Yes. Isn't that enough?"

"It's very faint, almost nonexistent. Part of the circle, just one letter of the place, and a barely legible *SE* for September. It's one of the old style of postmarks."

"I see. They often are almost illegible these days. Well, if you would care to bring it round—"

"I feel very cheeky. Of course I'll pay you for your time."

"Mrs. McNabb's daughter? Absolutely not. If I can help you, it will give me the greatest pleasure. But, Miss McNabb—that is your name?"

"Yes it is. Eve."

"I think you will not want to show me the letter. But could you copy down anything in the letter that you do not mind me seeing. There may be indications there—I speak as a policeman now, not a philatelist—that we could take with the postmark and we may get a step or two further on."

"I'll do that. Could I come around to your home? Or you come to me?"

"Come around here. I may need books and catalogs. I finish work at six tomorrow. Could we say seven thirty?"

"Seven thirty it is. And thank you in advance."

Eve rang off, somehow feeling greatly heartened. When

the next evening she rang the doorbell of 23 Butterfield Road, a small street of late-Victorian houses, rather small and depressed, and close to a monster-size roundabout, the door was opened by Rani's wife. She was holding a baby, and looked terribly young. There was also, Eve thought, a prevailing uncertainty, and perhaps an unhappiness, that mystified her. The woman opened her mouth, but she was forestalled by the door to one of the front rooms opening and a young man coming out.

"This is the lady I told you about, Sanjula. We'll be in the sitting room. I don't know how long we will take."

He was a good-looking young man—young, but by no means as young as his wife: perhaps twenty-eight or thirty. He led Eve through to the sitting room, furnished in a slightly ornate style, and shut the door behind them. He gestured Eve toward one of the easy chairs.

"I hope you weren't eating," she said. "I really don't want to inconvenience you."

"No, no—I'd finished—all I wanted to eat. Now let us have a look at this mysterious envelope—made mysterious by our wonderful GPO."

"Well, yes," agreed Eve. "But the writer didn't put an address on it, or on the letter itself."

"Presumably because she knew the recipient—dear Mrs. McNabb—was perfectly aware of what it was."

Eve suddenly gave voice to a thought that had come to her on a walk that afternoon, but had not been closely examined.

"That seems most likely. But isn't it just possible that she knew my mother was dead, that the letter would be read by me and that she didn't want me to contact her?"

Rani nodded, but unenthusiastically, as if he thought she could have picked holes in that theory very easily if she had thought it through. Then he switched on a strong light and looked at the envelope through a magnifying glass.

"We can forget the *SE* for September. Typically the most useless information is the clearest . . . The one letter in the place-name that is clearly visible looks as if it could be the last—looking at it in relation to the month . . . It seems to me it's a *D*—would you agree?"

"Yes, that's what I thought."

"And then—which you couldn't see with the naked eye—there's just a shadow of another letter here . . . Just a stroke crossed by—or perhaps met by—another, shorter stroke."

Eve was leaning over his shoulder now.

"Oh yes, I can see. But that could be quite a lot of things, couldn't it?"

"Yes, it could. I'll need to consult my books to investigate the possibilities . . . Now, what about the letter itself—the parts you will let me read?"

He said it neutrally, without a shadow of reproach. Eve took out the copy she had made of the parts of the letter she felt no qualms about his seeing.

"I've left out the last two paragraphs. Somehow it's too—"

"Don't upset yourself."

"There's mention in the last bit of 'the business with John.' John was my father's name—John McNabb of course."

"Of course. Women always took their husband's name

then, didn't they?" He took the two pages of notebook paper and began reading them. When he finished, he sat for a moment, thinking. "Pardon me—I should know this—but isn't *Hay Fever* a pretty well-known play?"

"Yes. It's Noël Coward. Dating from 1925 or so—it's a very twenties play. They would have to be very good amateurs to bring it off."

"When did Noël Coward die?"

"Oh, 1970 or thereabouts." Eve was bemused. "Why do you ask?"

"Still in copyright. They would have to get permission and pay a fee to his publisher or agent, and the money would go to his heir. I think if you got in touch with his publishers, you would find they probably keep records."

Eve looked at him.

"What's the matter?" he asked.

"All of a sudden there's a road ahead."

Rani looked shy.

"It was really very simple."

"Not to me. It'll be Samuel French or one of those play publishers."

"Phone them. Tell them you're the secretary to a new amateur drama group, and you're thinking of putting on *Hay Fever*. You want to know if any amateur or professional group has put it on in West Yorkshire in the last year or two."

"Perhaps I shouldn't mention Yorkshire, though. She could have been talking about anywhere."

"That's true. But if it's a popular play with amateurs, you could get a whole string of names and places. You'll have to play it by ear."

"I think I shall enjoy doing that. How long do you need to look at the postmark?"

"I'm off tomorrow. And if you ring the publisher of *Hay Fever* tomorrow, we could confer in the evening. The point is, the two things go together. There could be a large number of places whose names could fit in with the postmark, but the play and the groups that want to put it on may tell us which one it is likely to be."

"Could you come to me? Then we wouldn't be interrupting domestic routines."

Rani seemed to be about to say something, then just murmured that he would like that, and noted down the address and time. On her way back to the car, Eve was conscious of a spring in her step and a feeling of promise even in the darkness of the autumn night.

The next day she went early into Halifax, went to the library, and found out the name of the licensing agents for Coward's plays. When she rang them in the middle of the morning, they couldn't have been more helpful, and obviously were used to similar queries. A young man and his computer worked wonders in seconds.

"*Hay Fever?* It's up there with *Private Lives* and *Blithe Spirit* as one of the favorite Cowards. But we find that more groups say they're going to do it than actually do. It's fiendishly difficult—full of good parts that need first-rate playing. If you're a new group, you may find something a bit more straightforward would suit you better."

"We've got a lot of very experienced actors—amateur actors, of course," lied Eve.

"With *Hay Fever* it's a big advantage if they've acted together before . . . Let's see. Newton Abbot Players in

45

2005, Pitlochry Festival, Fishguard Amateur Dramatic Society—all well out of your region. This year Aylesbury, London West End with Judi Dench—now *that* was a performance—Penzance, Derby—getting closer. Oh yes: the Huddersfield Comedy Club, with performances due in November, and Middlesborough—performances this month. Those are the nearest to you. Especially the Huddersfield."

"Yes," said Eve. "We'd better put our thinking caps on again. Thank you so much for your help."

That afternoon she went to the one Crossley supermarket and bought several different fruit juices, some cans of beer, and a good white wine for herself. She was conscious of being much more lighthearted than she had been since her mother died—more happy than she had ever been, in fact, since she broke with Grant. "He's a married man," she told herself, "and years younger than you." But that didn't stop her feeling happy, and anticipating with something approaching excitement his visit in the evening. He was something different, something outside her everyday experience. In Evelyn Waugh's distinction between cars, between those that illustrate "being" and those that illustrate "becoming," Eve decided she was obviously one of the latter. She was always looking for experiences, people, destinations that could change her, develop her, deepen her understanding of herself and of the world.

When she opened the door to Rani that evening, she saw a very spruce young man, in beautifully ironed blue shirt and slacks, who was already smiling in anticipation of an interesting session. Her heart skipped a beat, and she led him through to her front room and settled him on the sofa with a low table in front of him.

"Fruit juice?" she suggested. "Or something stronger, if that's not out of the question. But you're Hindu, aren't you, not Muslim?"

"Yes, I am. But I usually don't drink. In the police force beer doesn't count as an alcoholic drink," said Rani, smiling shyly. "It's the liquid equivalent of bread— the staff of life. If you have any beer I would be happy— otherwise fruit juice will be fine."

When they were settled down on either side of the low table—and with every minute Rani's stance showed him becoming more relaxed, even happy—he showed an enlargement he had made of the postmark on the envelope. He had shaded in the two less than clear letters of the town name.

"Here is the month and day: all we have is the *SE*, but if the mark merely had *SEPT* it would leave plenty of room for the town name. There is no *D* in September, so it must be part of the town or region. Quite possibly the last letter, judging by what we have of the date. That leaves—"

"The whole of the rest of inside the circle for the town," said Eve, who was very competitive in quizzes and mysteries.

"Exactly. Therefore possibly quite a long town name. Now, this other shadowy letter: an upward stroke with another stroke emerging from its right side, halfway up. Most likely an *E*, an *F* or an *H*. I considered whether it could be a *P*, an *R* or a *B*, but I think that little protuberance would have to show a sign of curving upward, and it doesn't. Do you see?"

"Yes. It looks quite straight to me."

"So, a town name with a *D* to finish or nearly finish with, and an *E, F* or *H* halfway—or maybe a bit more than halfway—through. I could no doubt get an authoritative list from the post office if I used my police hat, but I'm reluctant to do that."

"Of course, I wouldn't dream—"

"I know you wouldn't. And maybe it's not necessary. The first thing I thought of was Harewood—an important place for Leeds. There would be the *E* in the middle, the *D* at the end. But I wondered whether it was long enough. And whether Harewood—in spite of the house, which must generate a lot of mail—is important enough to have its own postmark. Then I thought of that central letter as an *F*—"

"Field," said Eve, not letting on about her other information.

"Exactly. Wakefield, Huddersfield, Sheffield and so on. The position of the middle letter in relation to the *D* made 'field' more likely than 'ford' to my eyes. Otherwise I would have considered Bradford, Stafford and so on. I think there is room for more letters than eight."

"Yes," said Eve. "And I think there's something I should tell you. One of the places where an amateur dramatic society has applied to put on *Hay Fever* is Huddersfield."

They looked at each other with delight. Then Rani punched the air in the manner of a football goal scorer and they smiled and cheered, and wanted to embrace but didn't quite, didn't yet, dare. "One day" said a voice in the back of Eve's mind.

"Of course nothing is certain," said Rani. "But still . . .

That is what I love about my job. You take one step, make a provisional decision—always remembering the question mark that there still is over it—but then you take a second step, and that leads to a third step, and then you have one part of the jigsaw in your mind."

"Always bearing in mind the question mark," said Eve. They both laughed. "Is that why you joined the police force?"

"Oh, that's too simple. There was so much that I didn't know about the police force. And so much that I thought I knew that was wrong. But yes—I thought there was a lot about the job that was brain work, involving logic, step-by-step reasoning, and that was true. Especially about detective work. I have been a detective some little time now. Very low down in the ranks, but still—wonderful work!"

"And does philately call on the same skills?"

"Oh, I don't think so. Not logic, not in the same way. Philately just fills some time in the other part of my life."

Eve, feeling daring, could not stop herself from fishing.

"Competing with your little girl, and a thousand and one other things, I daresay?"

"Yes. You saw my daughter? She is fine, and I 'love her to bits'—I like that expression, and it's so right." The air was heavy with unasked questions. He stood up nervously. "I mustn't take up more of your time—"

"You are not taking up my time. You are filling it when it very much needs filling. Please have another beer."

He stood there, plainly nervous and pulled two ways.

"Well, perhaps a fruit juice. I am driving. And to tell you the truth, I drink beer to make a statement, to fit in, but I don't like it very much."

They laughed. It seemed to Eve that they laughed a lot, and that was fine, unless perhaps it was to cover over things they could not yet bring out into the open. It was too soon. Their acquaintance was too fragile.

"It's cranberry," she said, as she came in with glasses. "I don't think you can make much of a statement with cranberry juice."

Something in her remarks struck a chord, or perhaps he had been thinking, weighing the situation while she was in the kitchen. Suddenly he looked up at her and in his eyes there was nothing but misery.

"You knew, didn't you? When you came to my house? You sensed something?"

Eve shifted in her chair.

"Well, 'didn't sense' is more like. I didn't sense happiness. I felt tension, felt apartness."

"All of those things. I'm sorry. I don't want to burden—"

"You wouldn't be burdening me. I'm interested. I'm always interested in people. Maybe that's my mother's influence. So you drink to make a statement. Did you get married as a statement too, perhaps? A quite different sort of statement?"

"Yes. A statement that I was still an Asian, still an *Indian* Englishman. That I was quite happy with the rules and customs I grew up with."

"So it wasn't a forced marriage?"

"No, no, not at all, not for her or for me. Forced marriages occur, but not very often, in the Indian community. It was an arranged marriage, with a cousin from India. We had met. The family put it to us. She agreed. I agreed. She came over here and we got married."

"Is it England? Is that what makes her unhappy?"

Rani looked down at the table.

"Partly. She misses so much. She agreed to the marriage because it is the ambition of so many girls in India, at least in the rural parts, to find an English husband and live here."

"And what makes you unhappy? Presumably whatever it is makes her unhappy too."

There was a long silence.

"What makes me unhappy? There is nothing there. Nothing between us. They say it comes gradually. You grow to know each other better, then that familiarity grows into love—and trust, and mutual support and all good things. But we began with nothing there, and there is still nothing there."

"Except your little girl."

She felt she had to say it—the thought troubled her greatly.

"I love her so much, but she does not bring us together. She is a talking point, and we ought to be grateful for that, because we hardly have any others."

Eve thought for a moment.

"Did you perhaps go into the police force against your family's wishes?"

"Oh yes. They thought I should be running a shop or studying to become a doctor or surgeon. They still do."

"So was the marriage a sort of . . . compensation for going against their wishes?"

"Maybe. And me already nearly twenty-five. How could I be so mad, at that age?"

"It was the custom. You can't call that madness."

"It *was* mad: to marry when I felt nothing."

"And what does your wife do all day?"

"Sanjula? She visits members of her family. Sometimes too my parents. Goes out with other young mothers—Indian ones, of course. Her English does not improve, but then she hardly ever uses it. She keeps the house beautiful and clean, watches Bollywood movies, dreams of being back again where the sun shines . . ."

"Wouldn't that be the ideal situation? Well, not ideal, because of the child, but perhaps the best thing that could happen in the circumstances?"

Rani's eyes showed his shock.

"But then the shame. She is afraid of that, and would hate it."

"Why should there be any shame? Your parents made a mistake—"

"I tell you, there would be shame. Parents do not make mistakes. They have age, and therefore wisdom. Children make mistakes. They do not try hard enough. They have been corrupted by the wicked West."

"That's yourself you're thinking of, isn't it? Your wife doesn't know enough of the West to be corrupted by it."

"Exactly. But I do, and I have definitely been corrupted. Why else would I choose a job which is totally unheard of in our family? They have marked me down as a failure for that too."

"And are you a failure as a policeman?"

"No." There was no hesitation, and he smiled, with both pleasure and pride. "I think I have become a pretty good policeman. And that is not so easy when there is a tough and merciless minority who have their eyes on you hoping you will make a mistake. A *big* mistake. They have been disappointed. All my mistakes have been routine, everyday ones."

"Good. I somehow feel relieved that I have a policeman friend."

He looked at her sharply.

"Is there something you're not telling me? Some reason you would need a policeman friend?"

She paused and thought. "The reason I'm not telling you the full contents of the letter now is not that I don't trust you. It's that it's so vague, nebulous. I've no reason to think it's a criminal matter. If I do find it is, I'll tell you. But it's you we're talking about."

Rani stood up.

"No, it is not. I am much to blame. I should not have loaded you down with my problems. It is for me to solve them—they come from my community."

"Are you sure?" persisted Eve. "Are you sure they don't come from the fact that you are very Westernized, and your family wants to keep you in the ways and beliefs of their background?"

"Maybe," he said reluctantly.

"That attempt is doomed. You live in England, surrounded by the English."

"But there is much in my family that I love and respect."

"And you will choose those things and reject the other things. Your daughter will do the same, only she will embrace more and reject more."

"Perhaps." At the front door Rani turned and looked her in the eyes. "I do not know what to do."

"Couldn't you start by really talking over the situation with your wife?"

"It seems so hopeless—trying to make her understand."

"But you say she is not happy."

"She blames me. As my family blames me. As I sometimes blame myself . . . But then I ask myself: is this all there is ever going to be? Is this the most important part of my life? That is the part where I always hoped to do good. Bring up my children well. Make my wife happy and proud of me. So what can I hope for instead? Just emptiness. A long, long emptiness. Right at the heart of my being."

Instinctively Eve opened her arms. Equally instinctively he made a step toward her, and then his body seemed to suffer a great wrench, and he stopped and turned away.

"No, I must not, cannot," he said.

"That is for you to decide," said Eve, and there was a very obvious catch in her voice.

"You are quite right. I must act myself. Be myself. Do my own difficult work."

And he shot through the front door and disappeared into the dark street.

CHAPTER 5

Watching

The brash-sounding young man at the Huddersfield Tourist Information Office went off on a tangent immediately.

"Oh yes, we have amateur groups. And of course we have the Rep, and regular visits from touring companies—"

"No," said Eve firmly, hearing her mother's voice in her own. "It's the amateur groups I'm interested in."

"Oh . . . right," said the young man, obviously deploring her settling for second best. "Well, we have the Huddersfield Amateur Dramatic Society, and then there's the Comedy Club . . . I've just put up a playbill for the Comedy Club's next production. *High Fever* it's called."

"I think you'll find it's *Hay Fever*. By Noël Coward."

"Oh . . . You're absolutely right. I misread it."

And had never heard of the play, Eve thought.

"I'm about to move to Huddersfield, you see, and I've always been involved in amateur dramatics, wherever I've lived, and I thought I'd make contact . . ."

The young man smartened up his act, having been caught out.

"Well, let's see. I'll just get them on the computer . . . Just wait a minute . . . Oh, it's very slow—obviously going to be one of those days . . . Here we are. It's got the name of the secretary here. Would that do?"

"Do you have his or her telephone number too?"

"Her. We're very behind the times here. Traditional roles for women. Yes, her name is Edwina Fothergill, and the number is 01484 437 554."

Eve thanked him and put the phone down. She meditated over a cup of coffee in order to get her story in order, then rang the number. The voice that answered sounded like the actress Celia Johnson doing one of her put-upon Englishwomen in the 1950s.

"Four three seven five five four. Edwina speaking."

"Oh, Mrs. Fothergill, my name is Carol Dalton. I got your number from the tourist information office."

"Oh really? I often wonder if they've heard of us. And it's Miss, by the way."

"Oh yes, I—"

"After the usual messy divorce, I reverted."

"Very wise, I'm sure. I've been involved for many years with amateur dramatics," lied Eve, determined not to be diverted on to the messy divorce. "I'm about to move to Huddersfield and I'm looking for a group to join."

"We're *very* welcoming at the Comedy Club. Known for it. Unlike the HADS people, who are *awfully* snooty. With no reason to be. They basically don't want new people because they will take the parts away from the older ones. Our next production is *Hay Fever*, but of course that's already cast and well into the production period. It's coming on in November, you see. The next one after that, in springtime, is *No Sex Please, We're British.* Not my favorite play, but it always packs them in. Everyone loves a good farce."

Eve remembered reading that a great actor had said farce was the one thing that should never be tackled by amateurs.

"That sounds fun, at any rate," she said. "I'm in my late thirties, by the way, but I can pass for thirty at a pinch. I suppose you will have a casting session?"

"Oh yes, we certainly will. At the end of October. There's quite a lot of competition—*friendly* competition—for the good parts."

"I suppose so. The elderly actresses always seem short of roles, don't they?"

"Well, I suppose they are." Skepticism was creeping into the voice. "But when they say that, what they mean is there aren't many *big* roles, leading roles. There are lots of good, meaty roles for older actresses. In *Hay Fever,* for example, one of our regulars, who's done Judith Bliss in the past, is playing Clara the maid this time around. And she's finding *lots* in it, when she can find the time to come to rehearsals."

"And how old is she?" asked Eve, heart in mouth.

"Jean Mannering? Oh, sixty, sixty-five, I'd say. That's a *bit* too old for Judith Bliss. And anyway, everyone had seen her Judith. But there's no side to her, and she just auditioned for Clara. She always says there's no such thing as a small part. Trouble is, she's wildly busy in her day job."

"It's people like that that amateur theater depends on, isn't it?" said Eve, sounding intolerable even to herself. "At least I don't have a day job at the moment. Look, I'll give you a ring when I do finally move to Huddersfield, or to the area. I shouldn't have mentioned the move as definite because it never is with property these days, is it? Not until you've actually moved and got the money in the bank for the sale of your old house. I'll ring you and you can tell me what's going on and when the next auditions are."

They exchanged courtesies and Eve rang off with a sense of a job well done. That same afternoon she drove into Halifax and found the telephone directory for Huddersfield in the reference library. It gave a Mannering J as living in 23 Portland Gardens, Heckford, Huddersfield. She noted down the address and the telephone number.

That evening she was rung by Rani.

"Miss McNabb?" the voice asked very formally. "It's Omkar Rani here."

"I know. I knew the voice at once."

"Er . . . I want to apologize very sincerely for being a very poor guest last night. It was unforgivable to burden you with my problems."

"I didn't feel burdened. I felt I was sharing with you, and that pleased me." Rani had been speaking low, and in the background there were the sounds of men shouting and telephones ringing. "I realize you can't talk freely—"

"No, I can't. However, I wished to ask you not to cut me off from your investigation. It is something that interests me very much."

"That was exactly what I was going to ask you. I would like to have you on my side."

"Then we are agreed. But perhaps we should com-
municate by telephone."

Eve sighed silently.

"Very well, if we must, and if that suits you better. If we
are discussing the question of the letter to my mother,
there is no reason why you shouldn't call me from home."

"No, that is true. There is no reason not to call from
what you call my home . . . But I will also send you my
police card. I would have given it to you last night but . . .
events intervened. Thank you for your kindness, Miss
McNabb."

With the rational part of her brain, Eve thought: that's
one horribly mixed-up young man. With her brain's emotional part, Eve remembered how nearly they had come to
embracing, and a wave of tenderness for him swept
through her. No doubt they both were in danger of
becoming involved on the rebound, each wanting to fill a
void in their lives with something that had been lacking:
he was perhaps attracted to her by her maturity, her experience, her lack of silliness and shallowness; she was
attracted to him by his youth, his energy, his confidence
in everything except his emotional life. Nothing may
come of it, she said to herself. But she was quite sure she
wanted to know him much better.

Next morning very early Eve drove into Crossley and
told her mother's newsagent to continue sending the
Guardian for the moment, as she was unsure how long
she needed to stay in Crossley to put her mother's affairs
in order. In among the shop's detritus from the end of the
tourist and walking seasons she found a street guide to

Huddersfield and bought it. Then she set off in quest of Heckford and Portland Gardens.

All trace of the gardens that presumably were once there had long gone, except for little square patches in front of the Victorian and Edwardian houses. These were superseded halfway along the road by postwar semis and a few very new jerry-built detached houses with garages, some of them with conservatories glued on recently. It was nearly eleven o'clock. Eve parked her car near, but not too near, number 23, and waited. She very much wanted to talk to Jean Mannering, and had the letter from her in her handbag, but she was not sure she was ready to do it yet. She had picked up a couple of sandwich packs and a carton of milk on the way there, and she ate half of the chicken and bacon, drank some milk, and had one of her occasional cigarettes. She thought about what she was doing and why, about her mother and their relationship: had they really been close, or was there just the friendly familiarity of mother and daughter, without real warmth? But if that was all there was, why was she caring so much about what she had read in the letter? Most of all she thought about Rani.

After more than an hour she was rewarded. The heavy door of number 23 was opened and a woman with gray hair, wearing a coat against the early autumn chill, came down the stone steps, opened the gate and walked away from Eve's car and toward the little row of shops that she had noticed five minutes away. Her walk was straight backed, and she had passed into the street like someone making an entrance. An actress, surely. Eve was out of her

car in a trice and across the road, staying a suitable distance behind her quarry. As she passed number 23, she
noted that there were three doorbells in a downward
line beside the front door: two flats and a bedsit in the
roof, she thought. The woman was walking briskly—no
sign of arthritis or a failing hip. She popped a letter into
the post box as she passed, then took out her purse and
went into the tiny newsagent's and general store. She
emerged with the *Radio Times* and the *Independent*. She
kept on toward the shops, several of which had become
takeaways of various national persuasions. But there was
still a butcher clinging on till retirement age, and the
woman went in and bought lamb chops (Eve could see
the butcher taking them from the window). Then she
went farther, to what called itself a minimarket on the far
end of the row of shops. Eve dallied on the other side of
the road, and at one point she thought she had been
noticed: at the cash desk the woman suddenly turned
around and looked through the window. But then she
walked over and fetched something on special offer, and
went back to the cashier. When the woman came out, her
transparent plastic bag seemed to contain potatoes, some
other vegetable in a plastic pack, the special offer dish-
washer powder and some kind of breakfast cereal. The
woman began back toward home, but was stopped by
someone she knew—a man in a tweedy but perky hat and
a thigh-length mac. Eve had by then crossed the road and
lingered at the window of a secondhand furniture shop
pretending to sell antiques. The conversation of the pair
she was watching was as brisk as Jean Mannering's walk,

and she soon was starting up again. Presently she was back with the postwar semis and the late-twentieth-century hodgepodges, and then back to her own row of turn-of-the-century houses. Tripping up the steps without hesitation, she disappeared through her own front door. Offstage and into the wings.

Eve would have liked to get an interview with her then and there—to pop up the steps after her, ring the doorbell then sit down in Jean's flat and ask her what her relationship with her, Eve's, mother had been. Just to have it over with, to know, would have removed a burden—no, removed a piece of baggage—from her mind. But she felt herself miserably unprepared for a searching conversation with a woman who showed every sign of being on the ball. An alert, still-observant mind, with strong, long-held opinions—that was how she would have summed up the lady she had been observing for the last twenty minutes. She decided that talking to her was best done after considerable preparation.

That evening Eve rang Rani to report progress.

"Good evening, Miss McNabb," came his soft but decided voice.

"Good evening, Mr. Rani. I hope you don't mind me ringing you at home?"

"Where else? Remember you said that we are not talking about any criminal matter."

"Of course we aren't. Let me bring you up to date."

When she had finished her account of the day's events, Rani thought for a bit.

"You cannot be sure that the woman you saw was Jean Mannering."

"Well, not *sure*, but I felt . . . No, forget I said that. What I felt isn't evidence."

"No, it isn't. What you guessed is that there is another flat in the house, and perhaps a bedsit up in the attic. Of course you should prepare for the interview—if you get to have one—but not on the presumption that it will be with the woman you saw."

"Right. Point taken. Anything else?"

"Remember that the woman who wrote to your mother is an actress. Only an amateur, but apparently a good, versatile one. Even if you drop in on her unexpectedly, she may have a repertoire of people whose personae she can assume. Try not to attack her in any way, but just keep the talk apparently casual. That way you'll have a better chance of penetrating the mask, if there is one."

"Thank you. I'm sure that's good advice. How are you? Feeling better?"

"No. But thank you for asking, Miss McNabb."

That last exchange did not help Eve in preparing to talk to Miss or Mrs. Mannering. She could hardly keep the image of Rani out of her mind, especially his big, dark, hopeless eyes. By the next morning she had half-decided that this was not the day to drive over again to Huddersfield.

The morning post was showing signs of natural diminution. The people who had wanted to have their say on her mother had had it. But there were enough letters addressed to herself that she opened them quickly without studying the envelopes, and there was one that therefore came as a surprise. The address at the top of the letter was the Huddersfield address she already knew.

Dear Miss McNabb,

You will not know me, though I saw you often when you were in your pram. A friend in Halifax has just told me the news of your mother's death and funeral. We were very good friends in her early days in Crossley, and I do wish we had resumed communication when May had retired and we both had time to do things together. As it was we had simply drifted apart, and didn't even send the ritual Christmas card. Sad!

You have my deepest sympathy. I calculate May must have been about sixty-seven. These days that is a very early age to go. I hope time is beginning its healing work.

Yours sincerely,
Jean Mannering

Eve got up, snatched a short coat from the hall and set off for Huddersfield.

CHAPTER 6

Actress

This morning there was no need for waiting and spying. The house was known, the object was known, the approach was decided on. Eve got out of her car, walked purposefully across the road and pushed open the iron gate. The three names on the doorbell at number 23 Portland Gardens were Naylor, Dougall and Mannering. No indication whether they were single women, single men, or couples—probably for security reasons. Eve, oddly, felt quite daring as she pressed the Mannering button. There was a silence, then the clattering of slippers on the stairs.

"Hello. I'm not interested in buying—"

The woman was smiling, but impersonally. Eve didn't much like being taken for a cold caller.

"Mrs. Mannering? My name is Eve McNabb."

"It's Miss Mannering, and . . ." She blinked, and then the smile widened. "Eve McNabb. But I've just written to you."

"Yes, I got the letter this morning," said Eve. "Thank you. It was very kind."

Jean Mannering shook her head.

"It was a formal letter of condolence, and I did regret as I wrote it that it couldn't be anything more. It is so very long since there's been any contact. But do come in. Pardon me if I'm a bit nonplussed. I don't really know what to call someone I last saw in a pram. Eve? Ms. McNabb? This way—I'm first floor. Come in and have some coffee. Be careful on the stairs. They're rather steep."

They got to the first-floor flat and Eve blinked at the lightness of it: airy, sunny, with blinds instead of curtains and a general feeling of space and clean lines. Jean Mannering was well fleshed but also sensibly dressed—cashmere jumper, smart, olive green skirt—to make the best of her mature figure. Her face was round, cheerful and had probably been, when she was a young woman, decidedly attractive. Eve felt she was someone she could be comfortable with. She could smell the coffee, and it soon arrived with a plate of biscuits. So far so normal.

"You must be so busy," said Jean, sitting down and gesturing toward the other armchair. "I remember from my own mother's death—just the cleaning out and sorting was horrendous. And it was down south, so I was in foreign territory."

"And there are all the letters. I don't like replying with a form letter, but I may have to."

"Well, don't even bother with that for me. You will have got a lot because your mother was a public figure—and a very popular one. Your visit is the best possible reply I could have."

Eve took a biscuit and began to relax.

"It's very nice to talk to one of my mother's friends from long ago. I've found since arriving back in Crossley that there's an awful lot that happened that I know nothing about."

"Of course there is! When do we start having memories, after all? When we're about five, I suppose. And then the memories as like as not are of trivial things, trivial events, rather than important ones. My grandparents died in a car crash when I was seven, and I have no memory of that at all. But I have a sharp picture in my mind of a skirt I was bought at Marks and Spencer's when I was six."

"Luckily there are lots of people in Crossley who can fill me in about my mother," Eve went on, "especially on school matters. And there are neighbors, long-standing ones, who know things I don't. You never taught at Black-field Road, did you?"

"Me?" said Jean, with an expression of horror. "I never taught anywhere. I just grew up in Crossley because my parents kept the village shop there. Long since gone, of course. I got to know May when I was working in the local Inland Revenue office in Halifax, and commuting to and from Crossley every day."

Eve thought.

"You say you got to know May. Not May and John? Didn't you get to know my father?"

"John? Oh yes, I got to know him. Though perhaps *know* is too strong a word. We'd go to the local sometimes of an evening, maybe even drive out for a pub meal. He was around the house if I went there, maybe thinking up the bubble for the next day's cartoon. That was about it really."

"Do you mean that my mother was the dominant partner?"

Jean looked surprised that she needed to ask.

"Oh, I should think so. No: I know so. You could simply tell in all their exchanges, in the way they organized their lives. John was probably the prime earner in the household: teachers were even worse paid then than they are now. John had his regular cartoon shot in the *Glasgow Tribune,* and he did a political cartoon for them quite often, when something struck home. He did a whole series of hard-hitting ones at the time of the Profumo affair, which were still being shown around years later when they both came to Crossley. He was technically a freelance, and was published all over, but he was still close to the *Tribune.* I remember that he occasionally did comment pieces—he was an artist first, but a writer second. In spite of all that, it was always May who made the decisions. That was her nature, I suppose. And his to accept it."

"Did they marry after she came down to Crossley?"

"Oh no. They were married long before that, and you were not born until later. She'd stressed in interviews that they were anxious to have a child, and that John would be a sort of house husband and father. That was to show you were not going to be neglected, but I bet it fazed some of the governors! But she carried all before her. I wouldn't describe it as just by force of character. She didn't hector or bully—not then or ever. It was the force of her integrity. She was so obviously in love with her job, regarded it as a sort of mission. But there are other people closer to her at work who can tell you about that side of her life better than I can."

"Yes, of course there are," said Eve, wondering how Jean knew so much. "I was particularly interested in what you said about her home life—her marriage, for instance."

"As I mentioned, I can't really tell you much about that because I didn't see a lot of it. Often John was away in Glasgow—the paper insisted on that. Or often we—May and I—would go out together to concerts, or maybe have a meal together, all the different things that young people liked to do then."

"It's a long time ago," said Eve neutrally. She was skeptical: was this really what the young women liked to go around doing in about 1970? "I was talking at the funeral to the only other family member there—Aunt Ada we called her, though she was really my mother's cousin."

"Aunt Ada . . . *Ada*. Not a name you hear nowadays. It rings a vague bell. Was she a rather nasty and silly person?"

"Yes, I think she probably is."

"*Is*, I should have said. There was at the time one of May's relations who somehow got the idea that May and I were lesbians. That wouldn't be her, would it?"

"I rather think it would."

Jean became lost in reminiscent thought.

"She had a quite extraordinary obsession about it. Actually followed us sometimes—to watch what we were doing. Once we realized it we put on a bit of a show for her. Then May got scared that she might be reporting back to the school governors, or the Halifax Council's Education Committee, so we stopped that. I can't imagine what Ada would be like as an old woman. Or rather, I can, but I prefer not to."

"Not a pretty sight. Not a pretty listen either. There certainly is an obsession or two at work there, not just about lesbians, I suspect, but pretty much anyone who steps outside the general run. I got no sense at all that she'd talked to the local bigwigs about this, but there was a mention of my granddad—May's father. She didn't say she'd told him of her suspicions, quite the reverse: I think she implied she had got her suspicions from him. But that could be a cover-up. She may well have reported to him."

Jean stretched her mouth in distaste.

"All this seems quite extraordinary, so many years on."

"Yes, doesn't it?"

"And I think I do understand why you wanted to talk to me."

"I hope so. I feel it's an intrusion, but I hope it's a justified one. And there was something else."

"Something else?" Was there a new tension in that plump, comfortable body sitting opposite her?

"I'd got a letter several days before the funeral." Eve rummaged in her pocket. She had brought only the first page of the letter, not wanting to show her hand too clearly, and particularly anxious not to bring into the open the mentions of what was done to "John." She handed the page over, and Jean Mannering spent some time studying it. Finally she put it down on the table.

"Was my name at the end of this?"

"The name was 'Jean,' yes."

"No surname or address?"

"No, not anywhere."

"But it's not my handwriting, you know."

"It's very like it."

"Yes. All girls of my generation were taught to write in this standard upright legible way. I suppose they were all destined for useful but not particularly important jobs where legibility was a definite plus: secretaries, schoolteachers. I remember your mother's hand was pretty similar. Do you have the letter I wrote to you yesterday?"

"I think so." Eve rummaged again in her handbag. "Yes, here it is. I haven't compared them, because it only came this morning. But it looks very similar."

"At first glance it does. But look at the *ts* on this letter: I never have the loop at the bottom: my *ts* are always straight down and cut off from the next letter. And this letter always does a Greek *e* in certain positions—after an *s*, for example." She got up and went to the desk. "Look, this is a letter I'm in the middle of writing to the bishop. That's the writing of the letter you got this morning. Compare it to the first letter. That was not written by me."

"But it is from someone who knows about you, isn't it?"

"Apparently so, yes. I don't like the thought of that. I presume the first word on the next page is 'dramatics,' isn't it?"

"It is. She—this person, I should say—knows parts you have played."

"Does she or he? A Huddersfield person? It could be a 'he,' you know. It's perfectly easy to imitate a standard woman's style of handwriting—much easier than a man's, which aims at originality, forcefulness, things like that."

"Yes, I suppose it is. Have you any idea who might have done this?"

"None at all. Aunt Ada occurs to mind."

"Yes, I've thought of her. But it's a clever letter. It gets the tone right. I don't think Aunt Ada is a clever person. She would let her prejudices, her distaste, filter into the letter, and it doesn't."

Jean thought.

"The letter writer's not always right, you know. For instance, May and I had not been in regular correspondence for years."

"But she wanted to convince me—she surely wrote knowing May was dead and it would be I who read it—that it was part of a continuing relationship."

"That does suggest Aunt Ada." Jean looked suddenly and shrewdly at Eve. "But there was something else, wasn't there, in the letter. Something you haven't told me."

Eve now didn't hesitate.

"Yes . . . There is a passage of reminiscence about a lesbian affair."

"A lesbian affair we'd once had, May and I?"

"Yes."

"Absolute nonsense," said Jean, with authority in her voice. "But we seem to come back to Aunt Ada again."

"It does seem like that. Do you mind telling me: are you a lesbian?"

Jean's mouth puckered up into a moue.

"Do we have to? Oh well, yes. I've had lesbian relationships. But not one with your mother."

"Why not?"

"Isn't it obvious? She wasn't that way inclined." There was something intense, almost fanatical, about her tone of voice that suggested rejection still rankled. "Can we recap? I need to know exactly the situation. After your mother's death you received a letter from someone called Jean who apparently thought May, your mother, was still alive. That letter purports to be from me, or at least contains information that could lead someone to think it was from me, and it described lesbian—what?—practices?"

"More situations."

"Right. So what we have here is someone—probably quite old, and male just as possibly as female—who has an obsession about lesbians, and probably gays as well, who knew about May and me and our friendship in the past, knew about my small successes in amateur drama, and—what? Wanted to make trouble?"

"Maybe. If that was it, I wonder why she didn't write directly to me."

"Someone with a sense of drama as well as of mischief. Someone who likes to go at things indirectly. So who could it be? All I can think of is Aunt Ada, but indirect she isn't. And I suppose there's the possibility of your father."

Eve gaped at her.

"I was always told he was dead."

"Always? Since when?"

"Since as long as I can remember. I suppose since I was about five or six."

"Well, I have no way of knowing if he's alive or dead, but might there be reasons why she, May, preferred to consign him to the graveyard rather than admit separation or divorce?"

Eve thought.

"It meant I was never curious to see or meet him."

"Exactly."

"It seems rather extreme to suggest that he was dead if

he wasn't. And my mother was not an extreme sort of person . . . You've missed out one possibility, by the way: that you wrote the letter, genuinely thinking that my mother was still alive."

Jean Mannering looked at her pityingly. Eve had a strong sense of reactions practiced in advance, perhaps by someone who accepts the popular image of an actress.

"Eve, you may feel you have to consider that possibility, but I don't. I know I didn't. And I think if you go further into this, if you agree that the handwriting isn't mine, and that I haven't had any contact with your mother for many, many years—almost as many as your age, I would guess—then you'll see that the idea is a nonstarter."

"I expect you're right." Eve got up, and Jean Mannering followed her lead sharply. "I really should apologize for coming to see you, and for practically accusing you of— something, I'm not sure what."

"Don't mention it." She went again to the desk. "Let me give you my personal phone number, in case you want to get in touch again. The one in the book is for the professional me. And thank you: you've given a little bit of spice to an otherwise pretty routine sort of existence."

Eve wondered how sincere she was.

"I suppose my mother would have found retirement pretty dull."

"Don't you believe it. She would have gone on committees, organized a Crossley Festival, taken up watercolor painting, stood for the local council if you have one. That was the May that I knew anyway."

"That was a long time ago. But you're quite right."

"And what about you?" Jean Mannering's eyes were fixed on Eve shrewdly.

"Me? Well, I am wondering about a change of direction."

"Excuse my boorishness—I haven't even asked what you do."

"It's not very interesting. I'm a PR person—*the* PR person for a chain of supermarkets."

"Ah. Well, I can see that might not be the chosen life's work for a child of May's. How did you come to take it up?"

Eve had often wondered that herself.

"I suppose I fell into it, really. I'm good at my job, but it's not a job I'm proud of being good at."

"Well, remember: don't give up your present job until you've got a new one, and if possible a better one. I've had countless friends who ignored that simple rule and regretted it." They were at the flat's door now, and Jean let Eve out down the narrow flight of steps. Jean's voice followed her. "The only thing I remember about your father's leaving you and May was that he was ordered abroad for his health—to somewhere sunny."

"*Really?*" Eve had swung around. "Thank you for telling me. You don't remember where?"

"I don't. Where would it have been at that time? The Caribbean? Florida? I suppose Spain would be the most likely, wouldn't it? Holidays there were common, though still a bit of an adventure. Worth investigating, though the fact that it was for his health doesn't suggest you're likely to find him alive, does it?"

And she shut the door.

Eve strolled in watery sunshine back to her car. There was something odd about Jean waiting until their parting words to hand her this piece of information. Or misinformation. Did Jean want to direct her attention to her father because she knew it would be a dead end? Or did she realize that she was bound to go in that direction before long, and wanted to send her haring off at a tangent?

Thinking it over sent Eve further into a state of doubt. Was Spain really the most likely place to settle on in a search for sun at that time? It was geographically close, but the period was the early seventies. Wasn't Franco still alive then? And even if he was dead, wasn't democracy pretty fragile there in its early years? Eve had the feeling that the British colonization of unfortunate parts of Spain didn't get under way until later. Her trust in Jean, her inclination to believe what Jean said, which had begun to be established in the first part of the interview, was beginning to crumble. Even the perfectly good advice not to leave her job before she had another to go to began to seem like a shove designed to send her back to the Midlands.

If Jean knew her job was in the Midlands. And that might depend on whether or not she and May had been completely out of touch with each other in the years since Eve's childhood.

That night Eve rang Rani again.

"I've talked to Jean Mannering," she said.

"And what did she tell you?" When she had finished a rather rushed précis of what had been discussed he said: "And did you believe her?"

"At the time I think I did. Or was beginning to. But

when it came to that last bit, I began to think she had been too clever. Why had she not told me about my father going abroad before? She easily could have done. And was what she told me true, or tru*ish,* or meant to mislead entirely? Even her advice about jobs I began to find suspect."

"What advice was that? I don't even know what you do."

"I'm PR to a medium-size supermarket chain. She advised me to get a new job before I packed in my old one."

"Perfectly good advice. Are you getting a bit *too* suspicious?"

"Probably. I'll try to guard against it. It was just that—oh, never mind. Rani, I've been going through cupboards and drawers and finding all sorts of things, but so far I've found none of the 'official' things I thought must be somewhere in the house."

"Birth certificates, passports, that sort of thing?"

"Yes. I thought they'd be sure to be somewhere accessible like a hall cupboard or a desk drawer rather than up in the attic, where I haven't ventured yet."

"I think you're right. In my experience—in my *job,* I mean—there are cupboard people, and they slip these official papers under something or other in an otherwise disorganized drawer, or somewhere in a pile of games. And then there are the filing cabinet, or just files, people. Is there a filing cabinet in your mother's house, by the way?"

"Yes, a two-drawer job in Mother's study. I looked at it, and it seemed to be mostly about school: photocopies of reports in the local newspapers about special days: mayoral or royal visits, parents' days and so on. Useful if I'd been writing her biography, but not much to my present purposes."

"Keep at it. Examine all the files—don't miss one out because it sounds unpromising. There's a real chance you'll find the documents all together somewhere there. There should also be deeds of the house and other things you'll find useful before long. Your mother sounds a methodical person to me. I'd be very surprised if you found documents like that in a black plastic bag in the attic."

"Right. When I can spare a couple of hours, I'll get down to it. I've started to worry whether my mother and father really were married."

"At that date, and remembering the sort of woman your mother was, I'd be pretty sure that they were. She was a cut-and-dried person. And the people who appointed her would have made sure that she was . . . Eve, are you thinking of giving up PR work?"

"I've certainly thought of it. Without, unfortunately, coming up with any alternative that appealed to me. I must admit I've got bored with the 'uniform-shaped apples and pears' and the 'fatless pork' type of newspaper story that I waste hour after hour on. But that's what you get if you work for a supermarket chain."

"It's just that the Leeds headquarters of the West Yorkshire Police has got its civilian PR office in chaos at the moment. Rumor has it that the man they appointed to head the unit two or three months ago is turning out to be a blabbermouth who will talk to the press about any and everything in the most unbuttoned fashion, with disastrous consequences. Now, nobody is going to listen seriously to a detective constable from one of the minorities, but would it be all right if I floated your name?"

"Well, the work would certainly be more interesting than what I'm dealing with at the supermarkets. At least I wouldn't mind going to talk to someone about it . . . On the other hand, would it be wise? When I'm poking about, *investigating,* on my own account at the moment?"

"Wise? *Wise?* I'm fed up with always being wise. Where has wise got me? Into a marriage which is no marriage . . ." There was a pause while he tried to calm down. "Though of course I would not want to harm innocent people, or distress anyone. And I would absolutely not want to harm you, Eve."

"I'm the last person you need consider, Rani." They were silent for a moment while they both reflected on what he had just said. Rani's frequent, obsessed mentions of his family caught Eve on a raw nerve. "Drop my name into the conversation at headquarters. But I may be away for a day or two, searching for any traces my father may have left of himself in Glasgow. You can leave a message on my answer machine."

"I will. Don't get your hopes too high. And good luck in Glasgow."

"Good-bye, Rani. Thanks for the good advice."

But what she really felt thankful for was that her feelings, and Rani's feelings, had taken a step forward, perhaps two or three steps forward, toward the light of day. And she was willing to risk the possibility that she would turn out to be his bit on the side, his bit on the rebound. She did not think Rani was that sort, a superficial and changeable character, but she was willing to risk anything if, just for a time, he would be hers and she would be his. But there still forced itself into her mind, often, the image of a little girl, and one of a bewildered, unhappy woman who was as much a victim of clashing cultures as Rani.

CHAPTER 7

Old Pals

It was two days later that Eve set out for Glasgow. She drove over to Keighley and caught the train to Carlisle that had begun in Leeds. She had done the journey once, many years ago, with her mother. She had been told it was "one of the great train journeys in the world" and she had dimly appreciated it then, and had not found any that toppled its supremacy since. She settled down to enjoy something she might not be able to experience much longer, if the mass sellout to air and global pollution continued.

The train was full of walkers, who seemed to Eve to be a race of men and women apart. They talked about their favorite pubs, ramblers' rights, points of special difficulty in the walks ahead and bed-and-breakfast places with notably unwelcoming habits. Eve could see that to find notes pinned around the bedroom with such messages as GUESTS WHO WASH THEIR SMALLS IN THE WASH-BASIN WILL NEVER BE WELCOME IN THIS HOUSE AGAIN was to feel unwanted, but the discussion of such horrors meant the walkers never once felt the need to look out the window at the majestic scenery through which the train was traveling. Perhaps they somehow did not count landscapes viewed from a train. Or perhaps scenery was not the point of their activity.

In Eve's luggage was her mother's birth certificate and the marriage certificate of May and John McNabb. They had been found in a file marked PARENTS' EVENINGS, which she had ignored when she first went through the filing cabinet, and with them were the deeds of the house, which her mother and father had acquired in the autumn of 1971. She herself had been born the year before, eleven years after her parents' marriage, which had been solemnized at the Durham Registry Office on the eighth of March 1959. Eve wondered what the connection was between either of them and Durham. Presumably it was John's childhood home, or that of his parents, because May had been Glasgow both by birth and upbringing before her father and mother had moved to Melrose.

The train reached North Lancashire, with ramblers getting off being replaced by others getting on, all full of stories, and all with emotions ranging from rhapsody to outrage. At Carlisle, Eve changed trains, and by teatime she was settling into her Glasgow hotel and looking for a place where she could eat alone without being chatted up. She was well acquainted with the city from childhood visits with her mother—shopping and art gallery visits after trips to Melrose to see her grandparents. She chose a restaurant, not too wisely, because she still got alcoholic approaches. Glasgow had changed in the intervening years, but in that respect it was unchanged.

She had contacted Hilda Wantage, the archivist of the *Glasgow Tribune*, before setting out, and they had discussed what she wanted. Eve had simply said she hoped to understand as much as possible about her father, whom she'd never known. They had agreed she could leaf through a few years' copies of the paper to get to know his pocket cartoon about the McTavish family, and also his presumably more ambitious political and one-off cartoons. Then she had asked for anything in the way of information that the archivist could find in company records.

Hilda was a comfortable, motherly figure in her early thirties. She gave the impression she would have preferred to be home washing her son's football gear or her daughter's ballet skirts. On the other hand she seemed excellent at her job, and had a selection of old issues for Eve to browse in, and assured her she had only to ask for anything else.

"Are they divorced then, your parents?" she asked.

"My mother has just died. Cancer." There was the automatic sympathetic shake of the head. "She told me when I was a child that my father was dead, and I've no reason to disbelieve her."

But you do, Eve saw that Hilda was saying to herself.

"Well, I've found nothing in the records, one way or the other," she said. "He was employed on a contract basis, and he ended that in June 1973 'for medical reasons'— unspecified, but I've talked to one of the older employees and he said your father had had a series of chest complaints and was recommended to try a warmer and drier climate, at least for a time. He said the cartoons were popular, struck a cozy note that was appropriate for that time, and it was generally hoped that he could return."

"But he never did."

"No. I've found no explanation or letter severing the connection with the *Tribune,* but there was no reason why there should be, since he was not a regular employee. Anyway, I'll leave you to it, but I'm around if you have any questions."

She went up to her desk by the door, and Eve settled down to her pile of newspapers. She suddenly realized that she did not really know what she was looking for. There was no reason why there should be any news item *about* John McNabb. Cartoonists, with one or two exceptions, remained in the background, and were simply known by their creations: people loved Giles cartoons, but they had no idea what the man himself looked like, or what kind of personality lay behind Grandmother and those fiendish children.

But in default of better material she had to begin with the cartoons. She found that the domestic ones appeared twice a week, usually on Monday and Thursday, but could be shifted if a sensational news item broke on that day. The look of the cartoons was unusual and, Eve thought, attractive: a mixture of sharp lines and wash. The humor was less to her taste, indeed at times it hardly seemed to be humor at all: Andy (the father figure) shouting to Maggie (the mother) in the kitchen, she invisible, he standing over the cat vomiting on the carpet. The balloon read "Maggie, the cat's no so fond of spaghetti Bolognese either." An early response to Elizabeth David's promotion of Italian cuisine perhaps, but hardly hilarious. Or, one

New Year's Eve, there were the regulation two children (Betsy and Jock) gazing at their father stacking up bottles and asking, "Dad, why do you celebrate Hogmannay when you say every year things get worse?" She thought the problem was the tyro cartoonist with too little experience of life to screw a variety of humor out of it. She jumped forward to 1963 and found the two children, still roughly the same age, standing outside a bedroom door looking at each other with a bubble coming from the inside: "Mummy and Daddy are just playing Profumo and Keeler, darlings." Not even marginally better.

Looking at more of the later ones, she saw that the traces of Scottish dialect in the early ones had been more or less abandoned for standard southern English as the time went by. Perhaps that was a sign that the cartoons had started to get published in newspapers south of the border as well. Or possibly a sign that John McNabb was only Scottish by name and adoption, and had gradually let his Englishness take over.

He called himself McCrab, both for the pocket cartoons and for the occasional political one-offer. These Eve much preferred. There was one at the time of Harold Macmillan's resignation as prime minister that was typical. The apparently failing statesman is lying in a hospital bed, with R. A. Butler at the bedside. In the next room there is an array of racks, thumbscrews, whips and gibbets, with masked tormentors at the ready and a line of terrified Tory MPs stretching far down the corridor. "I assure you, RAB, I have no intention of influencing the party's choice of my successor" the old fraud is telling the eternal political bridesmaid. Later, when the earl of Home had become

prime minister, the series of McCrab cartoons on the subject showed the newspaper's delight at a Scot succeeding
a Scot, along with a distinct implication that the man was
by no means so unworldly and untainted by ambition as
his reputation at the time suggested. McCrab was showing
claws, and Eve liked his work all the better for it.

But there was a limit to what she could learn from
forty-year-old cartoons, whether lethal or cozy. Before
lunchtime she was up at the reading room's desk talking
to Hilda.

"I've reached a bit of an impasse," she said. "I noticed
when we were talking before, you mentioned one of the
older employees. I think I might get a better idea of John
McNabb if I tried to talk to him."

"You might well," agreed Hilda. "He's perfectly compos
mentis, and probably willing to have a chin-wag in return
for a few drinks or a meal. Pensioners of this company
usually are."

She had turned to her screen and gave a grunt of satisfaction.

"Got something?"

"Yes. His name is Harry Fraser, and his telephone
number is 0141 7659 766. When I talked to him yesterday he was in the canteen—they never quite leave us, old
journos. We've got quite a bit on him in the records
because he was a regular employee. His memory is pretty
reliable, though you may have to make some allowance
for exaggeration and embroidery—those are in a journalist's bloodstream."

"I can imagine," Eve said wholeheartedly. "Did he
mention anyone else who knew my father?"

Hilda thought.

"Now you remind me, he did mention someone called Jamie. What was it he said about him? That's right: he said Jamie and he were John McNabb's best friends, one inside the *Tribune* offices, the other in the big world outside. I didn't follow it up because I was getting all the information I thought you would need from Harry. I don't imagine there would be anything about Jamie in our indexes, but you could ask Harry about him. Do you need to use the phone here?"

"No—I need a bite to eat and time to think. I'll ring him from my hotel later."

Eve calculated that lunchtime would probably be a couple-of-pints time for a retired journalist and that Harry might be too old for mobile phones, so she had a bar snack in her hotel and then went up to her room to make the call. The voice that answered sounded well oiled.

"Harry Fraser here."

"Oh, Mr. Fraser, you don't know me, but my name is Eve McNabb."

There was a brief silence.

"Now, you wouldna be John's daughter, would you?"

"I would, yes."

"His name came up yesterday, otherwise I'd no have thought of it. He's a long time gone, your da'."

"All my lifetime, almost," said Eve. "I have no memories of him. Would you be willing to come out with me tonight for a meal and a pint or two, so that you could share your memories of him with me? He left a great hole in my life that I wasn't aware of until recently."

"Aye, your mother died, I heard recently. I never saw the wee lady after she moved south, but everyone said, and I wasna surprised, that she turned out to be a cracker—just the best teacher you could ever imagine."

"She was, Harry, she was. A cracker. But it's my father I want to get some idea of. Did he have any other friends in Glasgow who might come along for a bite with us, and share their recollections?"

Perhaps Eve imagined it, but the silence this time seemed loaded.

"It's that Hilda, isn't it? She's been yapping. Yes, there is Jamie Jewell. He's still in the land o' the livin'. But I've no got his address, and—"

"You sound reluctant. Why the doubts?"

She could imagine Harry Fraser pursing his lips.

"We-e-ell, the truth is, he's no verra reliable. Takes a drop too much, and then another. Just talks awa' for the sake of talkin'."

"Do you know where to get hold of him?"

"Oh aye. Early evenin' he'll be sittin' in his usual place in the Highlander, swappin' tips for tomorrow's racin'. If I can lay hold o' him, I suppose I could get him along to you, supposin' he's not already on to his third pint and on the road to bein' totally useless. If I do, you should be a bit sparin' of whatever he asks of you—and ask he will, that's as sure as death and taxes."

"Where would you recommend we went?"

"We could try the Spotted Hound. Food's their specialty, and they've a lot o' rooms—wee ones and medium-size ones, on three floors, so we could be pretty private, supposin' that's what you wanted."

"I don't know about that. You're the best judge. Is there likely to be anything come up that calls for privacy?"

"Naw, naw, nothin' in the world. Nothin' that I know of, anyway. But your da' left your mother and disappeared to Australia—you never heard from him again to this day, so Hilda in the library told me—"

"Australia!" Eve took a deep breath as she absorbed this new bit of information. "*I've* never heard from him. And my mother believed him to be dead, or told me so all that time I was a child, and after."

"Aye. So mebbe you wouldn't want all this to be talked about wi' too many prying ears in the vicinity."

"I suppose not. Look, I'll be in the Spotted Hound at half-past six, and we'll have a meal, and you'll try to bring Jamie along. Oh, and I'll get a table with a bit of privacy if I can."

She didn't, as she said it, think that privacy was a high priority, but when she thought about it she began to change her mind. Harry Fraser had had a slight reserve about him as soon as the topic of Jamie came up, and the drunkenness and loose tongue of the man seemed an inadequate motivation for it. In any case she was not inclined to think a loose tongue was a drawback in her present situation. Did he imagine Jamie knew something he, Harry, didn't, and that it was discreditable? Already Harry had told her something new, no doubt under the impression that she knew it already.

Her father had gone, apparently, to Australia—the hot, dry climate the doctor had suggested.

At half-past six she was installed in a snug little niche in the Spotted Hound, at a table with two empty chairs around it and in front of her a glass of Perrier water that could pass as a gin and tonic if the two old men were wary of speaking to a totally clearheaded person. She spotted them the moment their heads appeared toward the top of the stairs leading from the second to the third floor. One was clearly cajoling the other forward. When they appeared at full height, she thought at first they were both small men, but realized when they approached her that the one she identified as Harry Fisher was of medium height, but emaciated and bent. Jamie Jewell was five feet nothing-very-much, with a face suggesting a chirpy personality that was currently overlaid with reluctance. Eve conjectured that this reluctance was fighting against a partiality for free drink and food, in that order. They came toward her, looking like nothing so much as a comedy duo about to get into another fine mess.

"There's no so many lasses on their own here, so you stood out," explained Harry, shaking hands. "This is Jamie, and he was one of your da's best friends here in Glasgow, an' I doubt he had a better down there in the Auld Enemy."

"I'm very grateful to you both for coming," said Eve, standing up. "Now, what will you have to drink? Do you want to see the menu?"

It turned out they were both partial to the pub's steak-and-kidney pie, and each had a favorite dark beer. Eve insisted on their telling her their choice of sweets and went off to give the order at the bar, bringing the two glasses back herself. That was surely a couple of hours mapped out, she thought, with a refill of bitter if absolutely necessary. As she put the glasses down on the table, Jamie put his hand on hers.

"Takes me back, this does. I used to come here with John and May. Not often, but now and then. It warms my heart that you want to hear about your dad. Let me tell you this—he was a fine man, and don't let anyone say any different. I knew him for years and years. We met at college, in Manchester."

Eve had noticed his north of England accent. She had also noticed that his enthusiasm for talking about her father contrasted with his apparent reluctance to come and do just that.

"In Manchester?" she said. "I've wondered whether my dad wasn't maybe English rather than Scottish in upbringing."

"Scottish? Not at all, or hardly. He never did more than the odd visit to relatives before he came up here to live. Durham he went to school in. His mother was Scottish, so he could do captions in the lingo, and bubbles and that, but he was County Durham by birth and upbringing."

"But how did you both land up in Glasgow?"

Jamie Jewell frowned.

"How John did I don't really know. I expect I did know, but I've forgotten, just as all of us old codgers forget all sorts of really important things. John always did love doing cartoons and caricature portraits at college—did pocket cartoons for the college magazine, for example, and caricatures of all his mates as they sat around in a pub. If he wanted to carry on with that sort of thing, a provincial newspaper was the obvious place, with hopes of a London posting to follow."

"We're no provincial in Glasgow," said Harry genially. "Here's the center of the universe."

"Aye, well, it doesn't always feel like that. Anyway, he knew I wanted a teaching job in a good school, and he sent me any odds and ends he saw in the Glasgow and Edinburgh newspapers. I didn't fancy going to the sticks and being the only one around who spoke proper English, but when there was an opening for a good school in Glasgow I applied and got it. I've been here ever since."

"That was very nice of my father."

"I tell you, we were best mates. And he was like that. He was the kind who would do anything for you."

"Were he and my mother going together then?"

Again Jewell frowned. He was not joking about the memory of the old.

"I wouldn't be sure. A newspaperman's working day and a teacher's are quite different, so we didn't meet all that often. But I'd say I met them together pretty early on."

"And that would be—when?"

"Oh, darlin', I'm not that good on dates. The era of Supermac anyway. The prime minister who spoke to interviewers of his Scottishness though he was no more Scottish than I am or your father was, and never sat for a Scottish constituency."

"Did you like my mother?"

He smiled broadly.

"Loved her. A girl in a thousand. And so enthusiastic. You could see the children would just blossom, being taught by her. They'd learn twice as much as if they were taught by your average Scottish dominie, of whom I had more than enough experience in my own school."

"But you've stopped here?"

Eve had noticed his propensity for making snide remarks about Scotland and Scottishness, and she was intrigued as to why he had stayed. Perhaps in order to offend by making remarks like these?

"Yes, well, it was a good school. Still is, though the poorer for my leaving. With my height and my accent, I could be in real trouble in some schools, but this one— well, they were nicely brought up kids, there was always some real artistic talent there, and the ones who weren't interested did just enough to get through exams and inspections. I could have done worse, much worse. I had the itch to go to London after art college. Think what would have happened to me in a London comprehensive."

By now the two men were tucking in to their steak and kidney and Eve into her sea bass.

"Do you remember what happened when May got her job in Crossley?"

"I do," said Harry. "That was later. Wilson was PM by then—you can put a date to it mebbe. It was no a complete break, you see. He was around the *Tribune* office two days a week, so we'd often go out for a bevvy at lunchtime."

"Why did they insist he come back every week? It can't have been necessary for the McTavish cartoons."

"The paper didn't insist. He was a freelance. But it was by mutual agreement. He was getting better and better at the political cartoons, and that meant that the editor and the moneybags behind the *Tribune* were becoming interested in having at least one a week in the paper. There was always a political agenda behind the cartoons in the paper. There needed to be a weekly discussion on what the cartoons would be about, and also what line John was to take. He might not have liked the situation, but he was makin' a name for himself wi' them."

"So he had a flat in Glasgow still?"

"Oh aye, the old flat. A one-bedroom one down Mackie Street. It was getting too small for the family anyway, wi' the babby on the way, but it was plenty big enough for him on his own."

"You're talking to her, the 'babby,' you Scottish loon," said Jewell. "I remember you, my dear, the night before they took the train for Yorkshire. We had a small farewell party, just a couple of drinks, and we went back to the flat for a last one, and because we couldn't see them off in the morning. You were only a bump in your Mam's stomach, but you made your presence felt."

"How far gone in the pregnancy was my mother then?"

"Oh—just a guess: three or four months."

"And there was no problem with John becoming more or less a househusband?"

"None in the world. He was looking forward to it. He knew there might be problems when you were a wee bit older, but he was cock-a-hoop about it. And they'd fixed up maternity leave with the school in Yorkshire."

They were all nearly finished with their pies and their fish, and Jamie was long finished with his ale and was beginning to rattle his empty glass on the tabletop. Eve signaled to a passing waitress to bring their sweets and, after consideration, two more glasses of bitter. Jamie Jewell perceptibly brightened.

"John was a marvelous father," he said. "They both were tip-top parents."

"Did you see John much after he left here?"

"Quite a bit. His hours were more flexible then, so we saw each other pretty regularly."

"Things were going well with them?"

"They were, especially John. He was having the odd cartoon taken by *Private Eye,* he had a pretty good income from the *Tribune* and other papers that took the McTavish cartoons—all in all they were fine."

"Does that include May?"

"Well, I never saw her after they moved. John said she was loving the job, and later loving the responsibility of being deputy head." He took a second big swig from his new pint. "I can't think of anything I'd like less than being deputy head."

"*But,*" urged Eve. "You're talking as if there was a but."

Jamie Jewell went cagey. There was something else too—he looked slimy as well, Eve thought.

"Mind your foot, Harry . . . Oh, I never heard much about that. It wasn't John's business. She and the head didn't get on. There were . . . awkwardnesses. The head was a difficult woman."

Harry was leaning forward eagerly.

"I think Jamie is exaggerating," he said. "It was rather up and down. May was given a good deal of responsibility, and she liked that. But it meant that sometimes disputes about who was in charge of what took place. It was no life threatening. Just normal work politics."

"And when my father left the country?"

"It was no to do wi' that. It was medical."

Robert Barnard

"It was his chest," said Jamie. "He'd always had a weak chest."

Eve chanced her arm.

"It seems somehow an extreme solution to the problem."

"Does it? Sounds ideal to me. If a damp, sunless climate is part of the problem, then a good, warm climate is the answer."

"But an answer that means separating husband and wife?"

"I know nowt about that. Think about it: there could be any number of reasons for that. The marriage could have been collapsing before the change of scene was recommended. John could have met someone after he got to Australia. May could have met a man with more personality, more get-up-and-go than John had."

"Or a woman," said Eve.

There was silence at the table.

"You've lost us," Jamie said eventually. "I never heard of anything like that, and I've no reason to think there *was* anything of that sort."

Eve let it go. They were not the people to enlighten her about that part of May's life.

"What about the Glasgow flat?" she asked. "Did he give it up before he left? Sell it?"

"It wasn't his to sell. He flew out—that was rare then— as soon as he made the decision. He wrote to me from Australia, asking me to get rid of all the furniture to the Sally Army and give notice to the landlord. That was soon done, and I sent him some kind of money order for what his records, books and odds and sods fetched."

"Where did you send it?"

"Australia."

Eve had to stifle her irritation.

"But where in Australia?"

Jamie shrugged, again looking cagey and slimy.

"I can't remember that. This was thirty-odd years ago."

"Can't you remember which state?"

"State? No, I can't. It was all just Australia to me. Beaches, cattle, desert—that's all Australia meant. We didn't have all those soaps, making young people want to go there. I must have a leak."

He pushed back his chair, and almost ran toward the stairs and down them.

"There's a gents over there," said Eve. Harry shook his head.

"He'll no come back. You began to press him too hard."

"What else could I do? There was nothing very terrible in the questions. I'd have liked to ask him if there were any later contacts with my dad."

"You canna be sure he'd have told you the truth."

"Why shouldn't he have told me the truth?"

"Out of some kind of loyalty to John, mebbe."

"Are you suggesting he's told me lies already?"

"Who can say? I can't. But if there was something odd about the breakup of the marriage he could have held back things about your mother as well as your father."

"He didn't have the same long friendship with her."

"Long eno'. And you gave him a pretty good idea of what direction the questions were heading in. So mebbe he thought, I don't want anything to do wi' that sort o' thing. So he makes off into the night wi' his belly and bladder full, an' his loyalty to John intact."

"I wish he hadn't been so vague about dates."

"That may have been just one o' his fancies. He could mind perfectly well what happened when."

"I suppose so. Though in my experience most people don't."

"What did you want to know?"

"A lot of things. But especially when did John go to Australia."

Harry thought hard.

"I'd have said John left the country sometime in 1972 or mebbe three. It was spring, that I do remember."

"And how long after that was it you heard that he was dead?"

"I'd say it was about two years later, roughly."

"Was it new news when you heard it?"

"No. Remember none of us—not even Jamie, so far as I know—had had recent contact with him. People just began saying he was dead."

"No details?"

"No details at all. Just as if John'd told them to start spreading it around . . . Are you tryin' to believe your father might be still alive?"

Eve shook her head, but that was precisely what she was thinking.

CHAPTER 8

Changes of Life

When Eve got back to Crossley, she found a message from Rani on her—her mother's—answer machine.

"Ring me at work or at home."

Eve tried him at work—it was about three—and got him.

"Eve. It's wonderful to hear from you. How did things go in Glasgow?"

"Well—let me think: I discovered that my father went to Australia. I also believe—this is conjecture—that something about him is being covered up."

"What sort of thing?"

"No idea. But one possibility could be the reason why he upped and left."

"'Upped and left.' I love English expressions like that. You think there was some mystery about it?"

"I doubt if people with chest problems went—*flew*—to Australia back in the early 1970s. Plenty of better places nearer."

"Maybe. But a lot of old people won't go to Spain or

Portugal even now, even to somewhere like Benidorm: more English than Blackpool."

"Point taken. But I don't think my father was that sort of person. His McTavish family cartoons often satirized little Englandism—or in their case little Scotlandism. And he certainly wasn't old then. Why did you want to talk to me, Rani?"

"Eve, were you serious about the PR job here in Leeds?"

"Yes," said Eve, after pausing to think. "Not desperate to get it, but *interested*."

"I've had a word with the super who's organizing the rescue operation for the PR department. He paid attention. Like you, he was interested."

"You sound surprised."

"I was. Not because he wasn't right to be interested in you, but surprised because I'm too junior to have my opinions listened to. But they were."

"There you are—you suffer from low self-esteem."

"Ha! If you only knew me."

"Well, I look forward to knowing you better."

She was surprised to hear a little giggle at that. Then he became serious again.

"I say, Eve."

"Yes?"

"He said to emphasize that this isn't any sort of job interview. He wants to see you, have a chat with you, get an idea of your personality, to see whether you'd fit in. Very important after what we have just gone through. What happens after that, if he thinks you would fit in, he says he hasn't even thought about."

"Sounds fine and dandy to me. What do I do to set it up?"

"Phone his assistant. The number is 0118 2696 842. She's very nice—Catherine Peters is her name. Good luck."

Eve rang the number and they fixed an appointment for the next day, Thursday, at three fifteen. "He just wants to have a chat," said Catherine, and Eve said that would be fine by her.

She occupied the rest of the day in trying to chart the married life of her father and mother chronologically, but she ended feeling that the indications that had been given were too vague. Purposely so, very probably. Then she began thinking that her father's life in Australia—however long, however short—would surely have left some traces in the form of newspaper work. She contemplated going to the British Library, but then another thought struck her: the best stocks of Australian newspapers would be in Australia.

Why not go?

If she got a job with the West Yorkshire police, she could hardly take a week off as soon as she had started. She got on to the Internet and began to research the cheapest flights to Australia. She was not yet used to being comparatively well-off.

When next day she arrived at the Millgarth Police Headquarters in Leeds, she was received politely and was escorted by a very young-looking policeman, who must have been bored out of his mind with his duties, to the office of Chief Superintendent Collins, where she made pleasant small talk with his secretary and his assistant until she was called into his office.

He was a chunky, brusque man, with a spark in his eye that might suggest a sense of humor but equally might connote a ruthless pleasure in exercising power and clearing out the dead wood of his department. Eve guessed that he might wink at inadequate performance by his underlings once, even twice, but after that he would gain satisfaction in showing the sinner the door. He was, Eve thought, an efficient, cool but probably honorable man. He got down almost at once to the nitty-gritty of their meeting.

"What would you think would be the most important aspects of PR for a police spokesperson?" he asked Eve.

"I've only thought about it since Rani brought the matter up," she admitted. "I suppose cultivating good relations with the press while keeping one's distance—if that is possible."

"Oh, it is possible," said Collins. "The press understand the limits and constraints, though they're continually pushing against them. Anything else?"

"I suppose supplying them with the maximum possible information on a case without hobbling an ongoing investigation or—most important, I'd guess—prejudicing a future trial."

"Good. If you can get it, why can't—well, never mind. What about the PR person's relations with the police?"

"Well, I suppose that could be just as tricky. As I understand it the PR people are with the police—with them, for them, but not of them. I suppose he or she would have to start with the presumption that in a matter of controversy, the police have a case for what they do, that they must follow police regulations and so on. But the PR person would have to emphasize that since whatever-it-is has become a matter of public concern it is being fully investigated and the conclusions of the team going into the matter will be made public."

"Not bad. Why did you go straight to a possible cock-up?"

Eve thought for a moment. Why had she?

"I think people rely on the police, profess admiration for them, but underneath they rather resent them. Something similar could be said about the public view of clergymen."

"The assumption that they are holier than the rest of the population is resented?"

"Something like that. And I suppose policemen are like clergymen—a very mixed bunch, and after all just fallible human beings."

"You can say that again. So running a PR department in this setup is not like administering the staff of a bank, or a set of teachers in a school. They have to be near immaculate, but no one these days lives in awe, or fear, of them. We in the police have every gradation, from people who see themselves as God's administering angels to those who joined it to have an excuse for a good scrap."

"Difficult," said Eve. "But not impossible."

"Your mother was head of Blackfield Road, wasn't she? Crossley?"

"That's right. Did Rani tell you? A long, long headship. Did you ever come into contact with her?"

"Not in my job. I think there may have been some contact when I was there."

"You were a pupil?"

"It's not such a coincidence as you might think. After my father died my mother had to take jobs as housekeeper in families that could also house us children. The jobs never lasted long, so for a year I was shuttled from school to school. I'm afraid I hardly remember your mother, though I remember hearing she was a wonderful teacher."

"Yes. Like most wonderful teachers she was shunted up to a headship where she hardly ever taught. But I must admit she loved all the administration as well—let's face it, she loved the power."

"I think perhaps she taught my class once or twice when one of the regulars was sick. But the funny thing is, the person I remember from that school is the headmistress. And I don't suppose I ever was taught by her."

"So you were there *then*. When my mother was deputy to—I don't remember her name."

"Mrs. Southwell. Although I was never taught by her she ran the daily assembly, and I expect that was what lodged in my mind. Looking back I see her as an actress manqué. She marched down the center aisle in the school hall as if she were Marlene Dietrich—all eyes were on her, and somehow she always managed to *wear* something different or to *look* different—hair, makeup, whatever. And she conducted the assembly as if we, the children, were extras in a crowd scene."

"I had heard she could be difficult," said Eve. "Actually she sounds fearsome."

"To us children she was. Looking back—I keep saying that, but it's difficult when you're trying to see a child's memories not to use an adult's eye—it's possible she was slightly ridiculous. And I'm pretty sure she wouldn't have had your mother's skill in administration. In my experience people with giant egos never do."

"I suppose to you children she must have seemed like a fairy-tale character."

"I suppose she did. Something out of 'Hansel and Gretel,' perhaps. Probably today she's an aged crone luring children into her lair with sweets."

"Oh, she must be long dead."

He shook his head vigorously.

"Not at all. She was certainly alive—when was it?— some months ago. There was a piece in one of the local papers about her eightieth or eighty-fifth birthday. I don't remember the details. The face rang a vague bell, but as soon as I read it, and the name, it all came back to me— my months at Blackfield Road, forty or so years ago. She went on from there to a primary in the Bradford area."

"Shifted sideways, I suppose."

"Or even upward. It was a much bigger school. 'Generations of beginners will remember'—'her strong personality and her ability to make subjects live'—all the local newspaper clichés were there."

"Where was she living?"

"It was near Keighley. It sounded like a nursing home, or one of those places where there is a warden and help whenever necessary, but otherwise most of the residents can still do necessary chores and light cleaning and generally look after themselves. What was the name? It didn't have 'twilight' or 'sunset' in it, but it sounded like a last stop before the trumpets sound on the other side."

"Well, I expect I can find out."

"It shouldn't be difficult . . . Rani tells me you're looking into something in connection with your mother."

"That's right."

"*Not* anything criminal, he says."

"I don't think so. Maybe something underhand, something dubiously honest, or even some kind of trick. I've certainly not come upon anything that could suggest a crime."

"Good. Long-ago crimes get a very low priority here, I'm afraid."

"Even if the criminal is still alive?"

"That's basically irrelevant. It's the extreme difficulty of finding proof that is the deciding factor." He shifted in his chair, having delivered his little warning. "Well, I've enjoyed this talk. Can I get in touch with you at any time?"

"Anytime before Monday. After that you would have to leave a message on my answer machine. I'm flying to Australia to try to get a lead on my father. I'll be away about a week."

"Your father? Of course we always knew your mother as Mrs. McNabb, but I don't remember anything about her husband."

"You wouldn't, at school. But she was actually married when you knew her, I should think. After the early or mid-seventies she was either a widow, as she claimed; a wife in name only; or separated or divorced. I would like to know for certain."

"Well, I wish you luck. Though remember, certainty is always next to impossible, and sometimes undesirable. Your kind of quest is becoming quite common these days. They don't always end happily, you know. We had a case of someone who spent years tracing his mother, and when he succeeded he tried to kill her on their second meeting."

"Thanks for telling me, but I'm not one of nature's optimists anyway. I don't see everything sunny-side up—downside up, more like."

They said their good-byes, and she was escorted out by the schoolboy policeman. He had nice manners, Eve thought, but it seemed likely to be years before experiences like the ones the chief super had just mentioned wiped the expression of ineradicable naiveté off his face. When she got out into the street, she stood for a moment blinking in the sunlight.

"Eve!"

Rani was coming from the car park a few yards away. Eve wondered whether he had just arrived back at base, or if he had been waiting for her.

"Rani," she said, trying to erase any tinge of inappropriate warmth from her voice in the vicinity of so many policemen.

"How did it go?"

"It went perfectly well, I think. We 'got on' brilliantly, but I'm not sure how relevant that will be. All he knows about my PR skills is what I've told him myself. And that wasn't any more than a rank beginner could have learned in a couple of days in the office here. If he cares to follow up on my career, he should get a pretty good reference from my present place of work, but it probably won't give him much more idea either of me or my talents. Damn! I must phone someone back in Wolverhampton and tell them I'm considering a change of job and a relocation, as the Americans say."

"Is that definite?"

"It's definite that I'm considering it. Not definite that I'm going to do it."

"Well, that's a start."

There was something in Rani's tone that suggested he was pleased. Eve felt a leap of the heart, but knew she must go carefully.

"Rani, I'm going to have a meal out tonight. I don't know if you're on duty or if you would like to have dinner with me, but could you and would you?"

There was not the minutest pause for thought.

"I should be honored. And very happy."

Eve looked at him.

"Has something happened?" she asked.

"Yes . . . No . . . I don't know. We will talk. It's not much, but—"

"Shall we say Browns Restaurant, in the Radisson Hotel? It's a pretty conventional menu—English and proud of it, or so it seemed when I looked on the way here. I feel like that, though there's no reason why you should."

"I am getting used to ordinary English food. But for me it is still out of the ordinary."

"What time do you finish work?"

"At seven thirty."

"I'll see you in Browns at seven forty-five."

"Yes. Our first . . . date. Is it a date?"

"Oh, definitely."

"Then, Eve—would you call me Omkar?"

"Of course I will. Is that your—"

"First name, yes. Rani is my family name. It's easy and sounds nice, and everyone at the station just stuck with it. And Omkar sounds a little bit odd."

Eve had noticed the Radisson Hotel when she had been wandering around the city killing time before her appointment at police headquarters. Somehow the closeness to the town hall, one of her favorite pieces of Victorian overkill, gave her confidence in it. On an impulse she now went in and booked into a room for the night. She was probably making a big mistake, but if the worst came to the worst she could at least have a few extra drinks with her meal. It was nearly five, but on another impulse—she was going to have to watch out for impulses—she went and bought a new frock in the Victoria Quarter. Smart rather than gay, and needing another sort of handbag, but she hoped Rani was not the sort to notice.

He came into the restaurant from the street, dressed in the smart suit he'd worn that afternoon, but with a new and almost flashy tie. She raised her hand to him, and he came over looking appreciatively at her new dress.

"Impulse buying, Omkar," she said. "I'm just facing up to the fact that I am now the owner of a large house that will do terribly well in the next property boom. I am a woman of substance. I've booked in here for the night as well." She was so unprepared for the look of alarm that greeted her that she immediately denied all adulterous intention. "*Not* for us. I just didn't fancy a late-night train home."

"I could have driven you," said Rani, relaxing and sitting down.

"No. I'm keeping you from your family for long enough."

"Well, as far as that goes . . . But that can keep."

"What will you drink? Beer, fruit juice, wine?"

"I think I can still drive after a glass of wine."

They ordered their meals, a half bottle of red, and then settled down to talk.

"Glasgow first," said Eve. "I talked to two friends of my father. Lots of detail about his work, his circle, a bit about his marriage. As I told you I got a general feeling of something being covered up—particularly by one of the friends, a retired art teacher called Jamie Jewell."

"Any hint as to what was being concealed, or why?"

"No, not really. Perhaps the truth about his marriage. A slight feeling that it could have been rocky, before he took off for Australia, and something happened that was the last straw."

"Wouldn't you expect, if his marriage was solid, that he'd have chosen to go somewhere closer than Australia?"

"Yes. On thinking it over, I would. And I could see all sorts of reasons why the marriage could have been shaky."

"Yes. Surely it makes sense, if your mother was having any sort of lesbian affair, that your father could have wanted to get as far away from her and the partner as possible."

"Yes." Eve pondered this for a few moments. "By the way, I have found no evidence of his death, beyond the fact that people began spreading rumors around that he was dead."

"The rumors could easily have been true. He had chest problems."

"We're not living in the nineteenth century—coughing up blood, and Keats's 'that blood is my death warrant.' My mother died too young, but that's no reason to think my father did too, and *really* young. In a healthy country like Australia."

"Except the talk. And he didn't have the healthy childhood in the open that most Australians have. Don't get your hopes too high, that's all I'm saying. Any idea which part of Australia he went to?"

"No, I wasn't vouchsafed details. This Jamie character said he'd forgotten, but he's not the world's most accomplished liar, particularly after a pint or two. I didn't believe him. I must admit I didn't take to him. There was something a bit snakelike about him. I got the idea of some sort of trick, something that could have been a joke or a hoax, but in fact was deadly serious."

Rani thought hard.

"Does that thought come from these friends you've talked to, or from the letter? That sentence about 'the business with John.'"

"I think it comes from both, Omkar."

"Do you mean that something that might have appeared to be a hoax to the outside world was in fact deadly serious and had the desired effect of getting your father out of your mother's life for good?"

"Yes . . . I suppose if I had put my thoughts into proper order that is roughly what I think could have happened."

"And Jamie Jewell is still not willing to talk about it thirty-odd years after it happened?"

"If he was sworn to secrecy at the time—"

"It would be an oath that surely would have worn thin

by the separation of the two people most closely concerned. You think, don't you, that there may have been later connections between your father and Jamie Jewell, and he's not letting on about them."

"Yes. That's a possibility, isn't it?"

"Yes. But I'm not sure these two possibilities gel—the possibility of an apparent hoax, and the continued silence of Jewell due to an ancient promise."

"I think we're just going to have to keep various balls in the air, conflicting possibilities, until we have more information."

"Fair enough."

"By the way, I looked at his cartoons. Not wildly amusing or even appealing at this distance of time. But he was getting much sharper as a political cartoonist rather than the 'aren't people funny' sort of domestic one."

"Will that be what you look for when you go to Australia?"

"Oh—you've been talking to Collins. I'll look for both kinds, Omkar. I imagine the Australian political scene was so different from the English one that it would take a fair time to adapt that side of his talent. A whole new cast of characters to get accustomed to, a new political situation, with the states and then the federal government. I'd better get a good history of Australia when I get out there to get wise to all the major figures and controversies."

The waitress came to take their plates away, and Eve thought for a few moments about her strategy. Then she said: "Well?"

Rani stiffened in his chair, ordering his thoughts.

"Things seem to be changing. Not for the better in our

marriage, but in Sanjula's attitude to it. She is spending more time away from home. If I say I'm working late—something all policemen have to do quite a lot of the time—Sanjula takes the baby and goes to stay with one of her relatives, or even with my parents. She has a brother, happily married in Bradford; several cousins, mostly in Keighley; and she gets on well with all of them, including my parents."

"And I suppose that makes you wonder still more why the two of you can't make a go of your marriage."

"Not really—not now. I'd realized long ago that we have natures that simply don't mesh. Oil and water."

"Does she say anything about her visits?"

"Only that she likes the company. Generally she just stays overnight."

"What's your spin on this?"

"That she's talking to both families about our marriage."

"But that doesn't worry you? It pleases you?"

"Oh yes. Of course she's not going to win some of them around. My parents, for example. Sanjula knows that. But she's getting people used to the idea that things aren't going right in the marriage."

Eve's face twisted.

"Don't you think they know that already?"

"I imagine so. Of course I've talked to my parents. But I think Sanjula has taken it a step further. I think she may be preparing the ground for the idea of divorce."

Eve's face showed her bemusement.

"But you seemed so sure she wouldn't want that, Omkar."

"I think I was wrong. I've always thought of her as the naive little country girl from backwoods India. Do everything your parents tell you to do. But I should have realized people can't come to live in another country with another way of life without being affected by it. Little by little it seeps into you, particularly if you are a young person, and subtly it changes your way of thinking."

"And you think Sanjula is beginning to see there is no future in a marriage like yours?"

"I think she has seen it, and is beginning to pave the way for a divorce."

"You don't think she has met someone else?"

"It is possible. Or perhaps there is someone 'back home,' as she sometimes calls it, someone whom she would have preferred to be married to but was too weak to fight for when I was proposed. Who knows? And I don't greatly care. I hope she does find somebody."

Eve knew now she had to tread carefully.

"But you care about getting a divorce?"

"Of course. You know that."

"But I need to know whether I should care about your divorce."

He put his hand across the table and took hers. His great brown eyes were liquid, and he spoke softly, with quiet emotion.

"Of course I would like you to care. I think you know that, though we know so little of each other. It's what I want more than anything. But Sanjula hasn't brought her feelings into the open, and that may mean she hasn't made up her mind definitely yet. We have made one little step forward. Don't ask me to take more steps than I can. I have to be ready."

"Of course not. You're quite right. I expect it's my age. Old woman in a hurry."

"Don't mention anything so irrelevant."

"But of course it's relevant. I'm vintage 1970."

"And I'm vintage 1979. Does it sound so very much when it's put like that?"

"I suppose not."

"I think I should go now. Would you think it inappropriate if I gave you a chaste kiss?"

"I should like it very much, Omkar."

He bent down, reminding Eve of an actor in a period drama, and they enjoyed a brief, stately kiss. Then he stood up and left the restaurant.

Eve finished her coffee thoughtfully. She had enjoyed the kiss, and it remained with her as a promise of what one day might come, when perhaps she and Rani were a rather formal and loving couple, behaving impeccably in the public eye. Then she went up to her room, washed her face, and lay down on the bed. She looked around her. She loved hotel rooms, because you could be anywhere. But not in Leeds. She should not have taken a hotel room in Leeds. She had nearly frightened him. She was going to have to proceed more slowly, more carefully, more caringly. She accepted, almost gratefully, that she must leave the initiative to him.

She got her few things together and checked out of the Radisson. The girl at reception asked her if her room had not been satisfactory, and Eve said it was fine, but she'd

Robert Barnard

had a message on her mobile that she was needed at home. On the last train to Halifax, almost alone on it, and in the car on the journey to Crossley, she thought about her situation, and thought that, though she knew she had made mistakes, and would make more, on the whole she felt very happy with her evening.

CHAPTER 9

Old Head

Two mornings later, after a day to catch up on developments, to adjust her thoughts to the present position of things, Eve settled down to action. She was going to have to do something about Mrs. Southwell, the former headmistress—whenever a very old person was an object of attention, a degree of urgency entered the picture.

However as Eve was putting her bedroom to rights after a breakfast of toast, jam and tea in bed, she looked out of the window and saw that Mrs. Calthorp next door was already at work in her garden. She was conscious of having talked to her about the May they both knew—the middle-aged and the elderly May—but not about the young May. When had Mrs. Calthorp moved next door? She seemed to Eve always to have been there. When she went out of the back door and over to the hedge between the houses, Eve got the impression that Mrs. Calthorp was glad for an excuse to straighten her back and have a view of something other than ground elder.

"Hello—taking a day off today? You have been awfully busy."

"Yes, and I will be busy later today I hope."

"So much to do, I suppose. You're lucky you can get time off from work."

"Yes, I am. Though I'm thinking of not going back to Wolverhampton at all. Of stopping here, in fact."

"Oh *really*! That would be nice. Strangers always take a while to get to know."

"I wouldn't necessarily remain in this house. I'd like it, but it is very large for one person. Maybe I could let the upper floor. I'd still have acres of room downstairs."

"You used to have a . . . boyfriend, didn't you?"

"Yes. That's over . . . Mrs. Calthorp, when did you move into your house?"

"Nineteen seventy-three. I was carrying my second son—Jason. You remember? You used to play with him, nurse him a bit. You were about four years older."

"Oh, I remember Jason very well. So by the time you moved in, my father had moved out."

"Well, yes. He'd gone to Australia for the sun. Weak chest, your mother said."

"That's right. Did you talk to my mother much about him?"

"Well, no. I didn't get any sense that she wanted to talk about him. She shut down, changed the subject. People *were* still sometimes embarrassed in those days if their marriage broke down. And I thought she might be jealous of me, with a husband doing well in the world and a growing family."

"Yes . . . But I don't think it was that . . . When did she tell you he was dead?"

"Oh dear me, that's a difficult one. I think it was about two years later. Just mentioned it one day, saying I'd probably hear people talking about it. It was all rather odd . . ."

"In what way?"

"Well, when I asked if he'd be buried out there and if she'd go to the funeral, she said yes he would and no she wouldn't. She didn't want to take you on a long, difficult plane flight and she was unwilling to leave you behind. She saw I thought that a bit odd, as I say, and she said: 'You know we haven't been close these last few years.'"

"I don't suppose that was a surprise to you."

"Well, no it wasn't. I thought there might have been something in the way of a trial separation. But this was the first time it had come out into the open."

"Do you remember anything else about that time?"

Mrs. Calthorp thought.

"A little, thin, black band sewn onto the jacket of one of her suits . . . Going in to work every day as usual. I used to see her when I was washing up the breakfast things. Everything was pretty much as usual. Didn't she tell you much about him?"

"Not much more than she told you. I'm finding that my work here is trying to find out anything about him—personality, work, views."

"But why would you want to do that?"

"Because I'm getting a feeling that he may be still alive."

As she turned to go back to the house, she saw Mrs. Calthorp's jaw dropping. If she had suspected something about a separation, she had obviously not been suspicious about John McNabb's supposed death.

When Eve, in her search for Mrs. Southwell, got on to the Internet (the computer was not much used, she guessed, but waiting to be used when necessary in her mother's study), she found several nursing homes and residential care homes but only a few that seemed to offer to their residents supervised independence in small flats such as the chief superintendent had mentioned. The one that appeared to fit most closely Superintendent Collins's half memories was Autumn Prospect. Most people love autumn views, but here Autumn seemed to be a euphemism for winter.

"Yes, Mrs. Southwell is one of our residents," came a comfortable male voice. "Would you like to speak to her?"

"Yes, I would, please."

"Could I have your name? We have to be a bit careful."

"Of course you do. It's Eve McNabb. She might remember it. I'm May McNabb's daughter, tell her."

She waited, then was rewarded with a "Yes?"

"Mrs. Southwell, I don't know if you remember—"

"Of course I remember. I'm not senile, you know. Autumn Prospect does not take dementia sufferers. You're May's daughter. And you were named after me."

"Really? You're Eve too?"

"Evelyn. I suppose May preferred the shorter version to distinguish us, though to my ears it sounds a bit too biblical and penitent female." The voice was rich, but with a hint of stridency or aggression that now began to soften. "I was sad to hear of May's death. I did send a wreath."

"Of course you did. I had to think a bit to remember the name," lied Eve. "I believe you've recently had your— which was it?—your eightieth birthday?"

"Eighty-fifth. I'd lie if I could, but the newspapers all got it right."

"Congratulations, anyway—"

"Birthdays become just water under the bridge. So what can I do for you, Miss McNabb?"

She said it with kindly condescension, as to a young child.

"I wondered if you would let me come and talk to you about my mother."

There was a brief silence.

"That seems an odd request. You must have known her much better than I did."

"I suppose that's true, though I wish we had had more time together in recent years. The fact is, though, I know the May McNabb who was the mature headmistress. You knew the young one."

"True. But don't you think they were essentially the same person?"

"Perhaps. Or perhaps experiences changed her. But in any case I don't want to discuss her character. I want to discuss what happened to her in the years before and just after I was born—years when I couldn't know what was going on."

There was a much longer silence.

"I suppose that could be possible," said the rich voice,

now robbed of its stridency. "When did you want to come?"

"I wondered if tonight might be possible."

"I don't have a very full diary these days," she said, with a bitter little cackle of laughter. "You obviously do, or you're in a great hurry."

"I shall be away all next week, so I would like to see you before I go—if it's not too much trouble."

"Getting in before I pop off! Oh don't worry: everybody does it. You can come—oh, let's say tea time. I can't cook dinner for two—it's becoming chore enough to feed myself. It's number twenty-six. Shall we say four o'clock?"

"Four o'clock it is."

"Please be prompt. I don't like latecomers."

She sounded as if she was rebuking a child in year three for slipping late into assembly.

"I shall look forward to it."

"So shall I!"

There was some kind of implication behind Mrs. Southwell's last words. Presumably an old person in sheltered accommodation welcomed any relief from a diet of daytime television and regular hot drinks. But that wasn't the implication. The tone of voice almost suggested that, though she would enjoy the interview, she would do so in an unpleasant way. The caginess of the early exchanges had altered to something close to relish. Presumably, Eve thought, Mrs. Southwell had decided how she was going to handle the encounter. Eve somehow did not think that the relish in the other's voice meant that she, Eve, was going to enjoy the meeting.

May McNabb had a collection of town maps in one corner of an upstairs bookcase. Eve knew she had had meetings everywhere, particularly in other primary schools, and had needed to know how to get there. It was easy enough that afternoon to find Autumn Prospect, on a hill overlooking Keighley, with a splendid view of Keighley Moors beyond the nineteenth-century dwellings in the immediate vicinity—many of which had become nursing homes.

Autumn Prospect was certainly not a nursing home. It was a custom-built series of small flats, all on the ground floor, constructed in one large square with flats on three sides and a wall on the side adjacent to the road. It was entered through a single gateway with a porter's lodge, where a capable-looking man was pottering. He hailed her, and asked her to sign a book for visitors. Then he came out into the getting-chilly afternoon air and strolled with her toward number 26. As she walked Eve heard jazz on Radio Three and also the television children's programs. She approved of what she saw and heard. If she had to get old and of diminished capability, this was the sort of place she would not mind ending up in. Or taking her autumn views from. The sense of privacy within a small community was increased by the flats being divided into sections of five or six, with their own door to the outside world. The caretaker let her into the section, then took himself off.

She knocked on the door of 26, and there were sounds of movement from inside. It opened, and she encountered her mother's first and only boss in Crossley.

Evelyn Southwell was heavily made-up. As always happened, the orange-brown matte color made her look even older than she was, and the rose pink lipstick didn't help, or the gingery hair. She had a prepared smile on her face that Eve did not trust or like, but she let herself be led into a small, comfortably furnished living room, though each piece seemed designed for a larger space. Evelyn Southwell was walking with a metal stick, and she gestured with it toward a chair. Already on the table were thin-cut bread and butter, with dark fruitcake and currant buns. The teapot was under a cozy. Mrs. Southwell had assumed her strictures on latecomers would be heeded. When she had heaved herself down into the room's other chair, almost groaning with relief, she welcomed Eve in a fruity voice designed for a larger room, or perhaps an assembly hall.

"So nice of you to come. It's a great treat to see you again. It's not all of one's old pupils who remember."

Mrs. Southwell was taking the visit as a tribute to herself. And she had forgotten that Eve had never attended Blackfield Road. May had thought it bad for a child to attend a school run by her parent. In any case, Evelyn Southwell had moved on (or been moved on?) well before she, Eve, had started school.

"It's a pleasure for me too. A lot of people have talked to me about you in the last few days. You must have made a big impression in Crossley."

"Ah yes," sighed Evelyn with a flutter of eyelashes. "I always believed a good teacher had to be something of a *performer*—don't you agree?"

"Oh, I do," said Eve. But what percentage performer? she wondered. "So many people have passed on to me memories of my mother's early years in Crossley, and what an impression she made."

"Ah yes, your mother," said Mrs. Southwell vaguely. Eve sensed that she was being played with.

"And of course my father too." The old eyes, under the mascara, blinked, apparently in an effort of remembrance. Eve felt sure her namesake remembered her father perfectly well. But the woman pantomimed a sudden remembrance.

"Oh yes, of course: the artist."

It sounded better than cartoonist.

"Yes," said Eve, determined to continue with the subject. "I haven't found any of his artwork in the house. He went abroad for his health when I was very young."

"Yes, I remember now. People went abroad for their health then. Nowadays they just go for sun and fish and chips, or so people tell me."

"Many do. But from what I hear, Australia doesn't go in much for fish-and-chips tourism. I believe my father must have died there at some point."

"Yes, I remember people talking about it. I'd moved to Bradford by then—a big promotion to a fine, well-endowed school—"

"But you did hear that he had died?"

"Oh yes. Your mother by then was headmistress of Crossley. And people knew I came from the Crossley school. So of course they passed things on when they heard them."

Suddenly a sharp, sardonic look came into those old eyes, and Eve felt she was being directed by a cunning director of plays—forced to react in a certain way.

"But you doubted my father was dead, didn't you?"

"I didn't—let's say—think the news was conclusive. I

wondered whether your mother wanted people, especially you, to think he was dead. That would rule out your trying to find him when you grew up. I don't mean to be cynical, but that would have saved her an awful lot of trouble."

"Was my father 'trouble'?"

She shook her head, looking annoyed.

"I didn't say that. On the surface he certainly wasn't, and I only saw the surface. But death is conveniently final, and just being in Australia is not."

"What *exactly* are you saying?" Eve was getting annoyed now.

"Have some more bread and butter, Eve. Or some cake." She paused while Eve reluctantly took a small bun. "What exactly am I saying, you ask. Let me get at what I'm saying by going at it crabwise. When your mother arrived at Blackfield Road School, she was the answer to a headmistress's prayer. So wonderfully competent all round. I could hand any little task to her, and know that it would be done, and *well* done. When she became deputy head, I could do more of what I really enjoyed—teaching. And she still so young! In her late twenties, but she looked even younger. If she'd been in a secondary school, she could have been mistaken for one of the pupils, but in a primary school it was fine. She both fit in and yet was a leader. She was like a big sister to the children."

She paused, and Eve thought it time to step in.

"We were talking," she said, "about why my mother might have put it around that my father was dead, when perhaps it wasn't true. It seems quite unlike the woman I knew."

"Crises produce special responses," Mrs. Southwell

said grandiloquently. "Now the reason things started to go wrong for your mother—and they might have gone a great deal more wrong than they did if it hadn't been for me—was of course sex."

Eve raised her eyebrows, somewhat hypocritically.

"Sex? I don't associate sex with my mother."

"Children seldom do, unless it's too blatant to be ignored. How do they think they came into the world? I grant you that your mother, by all accounts, lived a blameless life for all the years you knew her. But it's those early years in Crossley you're asking me about, and while she was winning a great reputation in educational circles, and from parents and people generally, she was also attracting a degree of attention *from the wrong sort.*"

"The fast set of Crossley? Difficult to imagine that there was one."

"Impossible, rather. No, by the wrong sort I meant—well, it started when she gave a lift to Halifax to a girl who had missed her bus. I say girl advisedly, because I believe she was six or seven years younger than May, though she didn't look it, and I suspect she was quite as—or *more*—worldly-wise than May was. When May got back to school that day—she'd had a dental appointment—she was full of what an interesting girl she'd met, how the best people didn't always go to university or teachers' college. And that was the beginning of it."

"Was this girl called Jean Mannering?"

Mrs. Southwell was visibly disappointed.

"Oh, you know. Why am I wasting my time?"

"You're not wasting your time. I know very little about her."

Mrs. Southwell twisted her mouth.

"Bright. Talented. A bit of an actress. And a lesbian. That was the problem. May became quite erratic and unreliable. Where before she would do anything I needed done, without fuss, after she met the Mannering girl she became forgetful, or she would do what I'd asked, but in a slipshod way."

"Was this because she was having an affair with Jean Mannering?"

"I didn't say that." She held up her hand, as if to deplore an impertinent question from the class. "I don't know. Why would she? A young married woman with a talented husband and a new baby. But I think there was a lot of pressure, which left her bewildered, uncertain what she felt or what she wanted. I think she was torn apart."

"It sounds as if she was attracted."

"I hope *not*. I hope she was too sensible. Don't get me wrong. I am not against lesbianism. But I have grave doubts about that particular woman. It was all surface with Miss Mannering. She's done all sorts of things with her life in the years since she met your mother, and landed up in the Anglican church."

"Nothing particularly odd or disgraceful about that, is there?"

"I mean *in* it. As a vicar or parson or something."

Eve was extremely surprised, but her suspicions of Evelyn Southwell kept her from showing it.

"There are lots of female vicars now. I believe more women than men are going into the church."

"It seems very odd to me, after her having been in the

tax office, then business, and doing every part imaginable in amateur dramatics."

"Well," said Eve, "if it comes to that, a priest or a vicar is a sort of actor, isn't he? What he does in front of the congregation is ritual, repeating words he's learned off."

"Very clever," said Evelyn Southwell, twisting her over-pink mouth. "I would have expected May's daughter to be clever."

"So you don't know that there was an affair?"

"Well, I couldn't have asked, could I?"

"I don't see why not."

"Thirty-five years ago? In a *primary* school? The word 'lesbianism' was hardly known, let alone spoken. The nearest one might go was the word 'mannish,' and that certainly didn't apply to May, or to Jean Mannering, come to that. Whether or not there was an affair—and I wouldn't like to say one way or another—it was clear that the relationship was not doing any good to May's marriage."

"How do you know that?"

"Jean was around to their house as soon as John left to go off to Glasgow. Stayed there all hours—all night often. She and May and sometimes the baby, you, would be out to pubs, visiting tourist spots, going to the theater—as often as not leaving you with Jean's parents to babysit. To me, May seemed quite a different person. It was very sad, very depressing."

Eve could not analyze her reactions to Evelyn's words, but she felt that behind the words there was a sort of relish, a lip-smacking self-satisfaction that Evelyn was now "dishing the dirt" on Jean Mannering. Probably not even realizing that for most people of a younger generation than her, lesbianism was no longer dirt.

"And this all climaxed in my father taking off, supposedly for the sun, to a warmer, drier climate for his bad chest?"

"Yes, it did. You should ask the Mannering woman about that."

"I will. What can you tell me?"

"Not very much. It happened while both May and John were away."

"You mean she saw him off on the plane?"

"No, I don't. May was at a weekend conference in Birmingham about teaching history to the nine-to-eleven-year-olds. There were so many young women teachers wanting to attend that they provided a crèche, which meant you could go with her. She later told me John was in Glasgow on the Thursday, as usual, but he flew straight down to London because he was seeing a London editor on Friday—the old *News Chronicle,* I think, or maybe the *Observer*—about a job. London would have suited him for all sorts of reasons, not least because he was very English—hardly Scottish at all, except by blood."

Her voice faded, as if she was uncertain what had happened next.

"And?"

"The next thing people heard was that John had taken a plane directly from London to Australia. That sounds to me like Jean Mannering having pulled off some trick or other. Otherwise, why wouldn't he say good-bye?"

Eve thought.

"Why? Why Jean Mannering? Couldn't my mother and father have been in contact, realized their marriage was over and he took the plane to Australia to get right away from the situation?"

Evelyn Southwell smiled, not a pleasant sight. She had the answer.

"First, your father's going was the end of the relationship between May and Jean. If what you said was right, the relationship should have flourished. Second, why would he *fly*? At that time going by sea was much cheaper, and he was not a rich man. It was much healthier too. Third, if there was an agreement between your parents, why not simply announce it? Things were much more straightlaced then, especially for teachers, but public opinion had at least caught up with the necessity, sometimes, for divorce. I was divorced myself."

"Why did you divorce?" asked Eve, genuinely curious.

"I found after six months I didn't even like him, and certainly didn't want him near me."

Eve thought for a bit.

"Why do you think May didn't simply announce their separation, and the likelihood of a future divorce?"

"I can only guess. But the guess would be that after whatever Jean had done, May didn't want anything more to do with her, but she didn't want to accuse her of something that could become a police matter—might even have resulted in a prison sentence."

Eve had to admit to herself that this was possible.

"But you seem to be fixing on the most complicated solution rather than the obvious one . . . What happened next? Did May suddenly announce that John was dead? Had there been communication between them over ownership of the house? Or over the custody of me?"

"If there was, May wouldn't have made it public. That would have made it clear she and John had parted for good. And yes, eventually May did tell people that he was dead—the weak chest, which she'd used as the reason for his flitting to Australia. If he was truly dead, she took precious little notice of his death, beyond the announcement. By then John was just a memory for most of us anyway. We'd never had much to do with him, and 'cartoonist for the *Glasgow Tribune*' didn't cut much ice in the Halifax district."

"And I, if I asked about him, didn't harbor thoughts of one day getting to meet him," said Eve thoughtfully.

"Exactly. If John wasn't dead, he was as good as." Her old eyes once more gained sharpness as she looked to see if her brutal directness had wounded Eve. "If he was alive, she must have been terrified, your mother, that one day he might appear on the doorstep and ask to be reacquainted with you."

"Ye-e-es," said Eve, calmly. "And yet I never sensed anything like that. If I asked about my father, which I hardly ever did, she just answered matter-of-factly that he was dead. I never sensed that she was reluctant or embarrassed about lying, or afraid that one day she might be proven a liar if he turned up."

"But you know May: always cool, decided, unutterably competent. She could certainly cope with lying to a little girl."

"Do you think so? To my knowledge I was never lied to by my mother."

"Really. But of course there's one possibility we haven't

considered: that your father was or is alive, but *can't* come back."

She meant, this malicious old bitch, because of criminal matters.

"Now you are entering the realms of fantasy," Eve said.

"Not entirely. Your father could be 'in the frame,' I believe the phrase is, for something Jean Mannering dobbed him in for. If ever I met her in later years—which I did now and then—I used to make veiled references to your father's disappearance, and she always reacted rather strangely to them."

Eve raised her eyebrows.

"Reacted? Do you mean she responded?"

"Oh no. She's much too sharp an operator to say anything at all."

The feeble comment was accompanied by a malevolent glance. Eve got up. She felt distinctly hostile toward this old woman, but she was not sure why. The woman was still living with the feuds and prejudices of the past, but many old people refused to give up cherished hatreds. As she made her farewells and thanks, Evelyn smirked and looked at her craftily. And when she opened the door, she said:

"Do come and see me again. I have so many other, and *happier* memories of your mother, in the early years of course. And more of Miss Mannering too!"

As Eve got into her car and began the drive home, she felt quite bothered and upset. Evelyn's last remark (addressed to Eve, like the early ones, as if she were a child at the back of assembly) was no doubt true to the facts of her relationship with May McNabb: they had got on well in the early years, but the closeness ended when her mother took up with Jean Mannering. That was perhaps natural, but the way Evelyn Southwell had said it implied . . . what? Something like: that she, Eve, was muckraking in her mother's life, and ignoring all the good and positive aspects of it. Eve was quite sure this was not true. All she wanted to get at was the truth. That last remark about her having more to reveal about Miss Mannering suggested, if anything, that it was Mrs. Southwell who was the muckraker.

That evening she rang the number of Jean Mannering, unsure why exactly, or what she wanted to ask her.

"Halifax 342951."

"Er—My name is Eve McNabb. Could I speak to Jean Mannering?"

"She's in the kitchen. Nothing that can't be put on hold. I'll go and fetch her for you."

The voice was full and penetrating. Another actress possibly. And a lover possibly. After a second or two came a familiar voice.

"Thank you, Dougie. Hello?"

"Oh, Miss Mannering. It's Eve McNabb."

"Hello again."

"There was something I wanted to ask you. I've just been talking to Mrs. Southwell. She was my mother's head—"

"I know Mrs. Southwell. Though mainly by reputation. It's years since I saw her last. I'm surprised she's still alive."

"Very much so. And in pretty full control of her marbles—and of her long-cherished prejudices. I was told about you being in the church—actually ordained. I didn't realize that."

"I never tell people I meet casually. Why should I? A plumber doesn't feel he has to proclaim his vocation. But it's not something I'm ashamed or embarrassed about. It's a cause of great joy."

"I'm sure it is. Mrs. Southwell was telling me about the time my father took off—effectively ending the marriage, though that may not have been the intention at the time."

"I don't think it was. I do remember very little about it. I don't even remember where he took off *to*, though thinking it over I got the idea it could have been Australia."

"It was," said Eve. She had wondered since their conversation whether her mother's closest friend could really have forgotten such an important fact, even if, perhaps especially when, she and May had split up, for whatever reason, immediately after it had happened. "It was a weekend when both he and my mother were away from Yorkshire, apparently. He'd been up in Glasgow as usual, then flew down to London. My mother was at a conference in Birmingham."

"Yes, I seem to remember that—dimly."

"Do you remember what actually happened on those days?"

There was a moment's pause.

"Well no, I don't. I'm not sure I ever knew."

"But how did you hear about his being no longer around?"

"May told me when she got back from Birmingham. Said—let me see—that his old doctor in Glasgow had diagnosed a chest infection that was really serious, and recommended a warmer climate."

"Permanently, or as a cure?"

"As a cure, I *think*. And I should think May must have mentioned Australia then, though it went out of my mind."

"I suppose you weren't too upset?"

"No, I wasn't. His departure gave me the playing field to myself. But I want to emphasize that May and I had not then had a sexual relationship and we never did have a sexual relationship. Never. Whatever old Mrs. Southwell may have told you."

"Oh, I can take what she says with a pinch of salt. She's a performer still, and will probably get back to me with further stuff to prolong the attention. That's what she promised—or threatened. I won't necessarily believe whatever she says, especially if it's about you. She did seem to have her knife into you, to enjoy the thought of embarrassing you. But you don't remember any more details, like where in Australia he went, do you?"

"No."

"Thank you very much for your help."

But when she put the phone down, Eve was more convinced than ever that Jean Mannering's story did not, as it stood, hold water. She, more than anyone, must have been intent on finding out whether the marriage was interrupted, or really over. It must have been a topic of conversation between Jean and May, and whatever was said must have been unforgettable.

Yet Jean Mannering implied that a blanket was pulled down on the whole matter—or that her memory had wiped clean the slate. It didn't make sense at all. Even if as soon as she got back from her weekend in Birmingham, May put an end to their relationship, something must have been said about the marriage.

Jean Mannering, more and more, did not seem to add up.

CHAPTER 10

Antipodean

Three days later Eve sat in the main reading room of Sydney University Library, sunshine streaming through the windows, with only a few students and jet lag for company, and surrounded by the files of those newspapers that had not been put on microfilm and the reels of those that had. It was going to be very difficult to concentrate, she decided.

The jet lag, like the journey, was horrendous. Somehow she was still living with the mixture of boredom and anger: the awfulness of the food, the puerility of the films, the nursery-school-like organization of the passengers' time, where you half-expected the stewards and stewardesses to come around offering furry toys. Oh, and *The Four Seasons* on the music channel, the fear that the person in the next seat was going to start up a conversation, the humiliating gratitude when after fifteen hours of excruciating boredom he did.

She took up a weighty file, identified the pages of the newspaper where cartoons were usually printed, then flicked through a few editions from 1973. Nothing that remotely resembled her father's work for the *Glasgow Tribune*. She flicked to the end of the file: still the same cartoonist. There was nothing in the *Adelaide Observer*. She took up the *Newcastle Herald*. Same result.

She was six newspapers in before she struck gold, but then it was the real thing, not the fools' variety. The paper was the *Canberra News*—not a national paper, in fact, but a regional one, though one that naturally had a special interest in all the main political stories. By chance the file she had ordered was for 1975. On the leader page there was a large cartoon, in the familiar mixture of wash and sharp lines. It depicted a stern lady, labeled AUSTRALIA, showing the door to a servant girl carrying a baby labeled NATIONAL PRIDE. Eve flicked to the front page. It was the week that Gough Whitlam had been dismissed as prime minister of Australia by the governor-general. Eve knew from her spasmodic reading on the plane that this was an event generally regarded as a turning point in postwar Australian history: the moment when the traditional ruling class showed they would use any means to keep control. The dismissal was seen as the work of the Anglophiles, the CIA, the royalists, the big-money people, anyone who was the bogeyman grouping of some sections of the country's population. But whatever the face behind the backstabbing dagger, there was no doubt that Australia was divided down the middle.

Eve turned back to the cartoon. This was the sort of situation where the political cartoonist came into his own. The more she looked at it, the better she liked it. It was probably, she decided, a tad old-fashioned even for its time, and deliberately so. Though at first sight the picture seemed to present a stereotypical cartoon situation, of the "Never darken my doors again" type, the closer one looked the more subtle it seemed. From the photograph in her Australian history book, Eve knew that there could be no doubt that the servant-girl was Whitlam. Far from being the tearful penitent of the popular situation, this mannish girl was proud, carrying a priceless bundle away with an air that was almost stroppy. The figure representing Australia had some resemblance to the then-still-living and long-lasting former prime minister of Australia, Robert Menzies, whose period of office had seemed more like a reign than the usual spell in the driving seat. The closer one looked at the caricature, the more cunning and greedy were the eyes, the more ruthless and sadistic the twist in the mouth.

The cartoon was signed Pete Pomeroz. The surname foxed Eve for a moment. Then she remembered the popular word of abuse for British migrants, Poms, and the affectionate abbreviation for Australia itself, Oz. Was the onetime John McNabb advertising himself as a citizen of two countries, or as someone caught between these two countries? He seemed to have been affected by Australia's famed hatred of "tall poppies," the ones who thought themselves natural rulers, above the common herd. Remaining from the Glasgow cartoons, though, was the British fondness for indirection, for leaving meanings latent rather than spelling them out.

Eve was about to proceed further with the papers, trying to trace her father's career in the Australian newspaper world, however long it had lasted, when a thought occurred to her. She made her way to the inquiries desk, where, unusually for librarians, she found a helpful face.

"What can I do for you?"

"I wonder, is there some kind of directory for journalists, and other people who work for the papers?"

"I believe there is. Let me see, as I remember it, it's mainly an internal one put out for journalists, editors, managers and so on. To make contact easier if there is a news story breaking in Cairns or Broome or Woop-Woop. I think we're allowed to buy copies, because it's been used by other newspaper researchers." She had been tapping on her computer and now took Eve to a shelf in the far recesses of the library. "There you are. Seems to come out every three or four years. You'll probably find what you want in one of these."

Eve looked at the series of volumes, going back to dusty and rather homemade editions from the thirties, then on to more businesslike editions from recent years. Feeling greatly daring she took out first the 2005 version, the latest, and then one from 1979. She stood, alone, against the shelf and opened the recent one. There was no entry under McNabb. Her heart sank. Then under Pomeroz, Peter, the volume referred the reader to Coltroon, Steven. Hurriedly she flicked back, and was rewarded by the opening of the entry:

COLTROON, Steven (1935–)

Eve clutched at the shelf to steady herself. He was alive! Or was in 2005. It was a wonderful revelation. Or more accurately, a confirmation. Because she was con-

scious that this was only what she had come to believe:
her mother, who was by nature and conviction a truthful
woman, had nevertheless thought it worth lying to her on
this vital matter.

She read on:

> Born UK, emigrated to Australia in 1973. Began his
> Australian career with the *Canberra News*, producing
> a weekly cartoon, usually with a political theme. The
> distinction of his artistry and the accuracy and humor
> of his caricatures was soon recognized, and in 1979 he
> became one of the cartoonists on the *Australian
> Guardian*. His career there was long, and by the time
> he retired, his Saturday cartoon was relished not only
> by the paper's far-flung readership but by the whole
> population. Exhibitions of his paintings, usually fig-
> ures against very Australian landscapes, were held in
> Sydney in 1987 and 2001, and in Melbourne in 1997.
> His retirement has not meant the end of his cartoons,
> which appear from time to time in the *Guardian* and
> elsewhere. Addresses: flat 97, Manly Heights, Sydney
> (tel. 9257 4075) and 25 Bay St., Maconochie Harbour
> (tel. 2665 9721).

The 1979 edition added nothing to this, though it did
say under Coltroon that he was "one of our most promising cartoonists, with sharpness of wit as well as of pencil."
Eve thought it rather impressive that after only six years
in the country, he was thought of already as "our." The
Directory of Australian Journalism obligingly included a
map, and she looked up Maconochie Harbour. It was

midway between Port Macquarie and Coffs Harbour. Neither name meant much to Eve, but it looked like a day's drive.

When she got back to her hotel in the King's Cross district, she rang the Sydney number the directory had given.

"Could I speak to Mr. Coltroon please?"

"He doesn't live here anymore."

"I see. Does he live in Maconochie Harbour?"

"Yes, try there. Sorry to be a bit abrupt, but we get an awful lot of calls for him. He's a very popular person."

So that was that. Eve went down to the hotel lobby and ordered a hire car for the next morning. Rather than gain her first impressions from a voice, she now had a chance to meet him face-to-face, judge him from expressions, eyes, demeanor. At the very worst, if he was away, she could talk to his neighbors. Maconochie Harbour did not sound, somehow, as if it was a massive jungle of surfies and boaters.

The next day, early, she managed the escape from Sydney, which seemed to straggle to infinity, then pointed herself in the direction of the north coast of New South Wales. She stopped for lunch and a small beer at a modern-looking hotel, then took to the road again in a journey that involved to her right fabulous sea and beach vistas, and to the left sun-bathed but still grim-looking mountains. She slowed down, both to take in the landscape—which would never be *her* landscape, but was worth absorbing—and also to feel less of a frazzle when she finally arrived. It was late afternoon when she first saw signs directing her to Maconochie Harbour, and she pulled into it half an hour later.

It was, as she had expected, no aquatic superbowl, but merely a long stretch of main street just above the beach, with little streets going off it in the direction of the mountains. All these streets had small- and medium-size houses—bungalows, as she thought of them—some weatherboard, some more substantial looking. It was just what she had expected her father to retire to, though she couldn't have said why. At either end of the principal street, there was a motel, with two hotels in the middle. She had been warned to be careful of hotels, so she chose the newer-looking of the motels. No point in cutting corners.

"You don't happen to know a Steven Coltroon, do you?" she asked the receptionist when she had registered.

"The artist bloke?"

"He's a cartoonist, yes."

"Yeah, we know him here. Comes in once or twice a month for a meal. He mostly paints now. Down by the harbor, on the beach, or sometimes in the mountains. You could have passed him as you drove through the town."

"No, I think I'd have noticed."

"He lives on one of the small streets—Jacaranda Street, I think, though I couldn't swear to it. Maybe Bay Street. Ask anyone. He's a well-known local character—quite a national celebrity, people say. Has a lot of visitors."

"I'll see if I can make contact when I've freshened up. I'm not used to the heat."

Robert Barnard

"Heat? It's only the beginning of spring. You stop here till Christmas and we'll show you some heat!"

Eve kept her thoughts on a hot Christmas to herself. She showered, put on light, clean clothing—blouse and skirt, which seemed right for the climate—then left the Ocean View Motel and began walking along the main street, with its view, between the small shops, down to a sort of promenade, more like a stone edging to the beach. There was no artist on the street, but when she got a good view between two shops, she glimpsed a man with an easel at the other end of the harbor.

She slowed down to a dawdle, wondering how she was going to approach her father, if it was him. She looked in shop windows without finding inspiration. Eventually she had to come to an opening where she could see the man, but she found when she came to it that she could see only his back. The one photograph she had seen of him was of little use with only a back to go on. This man was of middle height, with most of his hair, wearing short-sleeved shirt, light-colored slacks and sandals on bare feet. He was looking out toward the sea—lightly misted, with dusk not far off. On the easel in front of him was the beginning of a painting. Her heart in her mouth, she took the little path down to where he was sitting, on a small stool a few feet up from the promenade. She stopped, and stood a short way away.

"Do you mind if people watch you?"

"Not at all," he said, in a still-rather-English voice. "Though I suppose I would if you stopped here an hour or two. There's not a great deal to do in Maconochie Harbour."

146

"But plenty to paint?"

"Enough. The problem is the light. It's so bright and complete, like an early Technicolor film—as if everything was lit by giant kerosene lamps. I can't do with it. I prefer to wait for poor weather, or till what passes for twilight in Australia."

"You prefer mists and halftones and blurred edges."

"Yes, particularly the blurred edges. The sun gives everything an edge so hard and definite. Though sometimes in the shadows of the rocks you can see wonderful wildlife, and capture them in sketches. The wild things here are so cocky and confident. They think they own the place, and I guess they do, most of it."

"I suppose it feels as if the people have just hired it for a century or two."

"Exactly. Well, be my guest." He turned and continued painting. Eve moved forward to get a better look at him.

His hair, though thinning, had been abundant, and what was left of it was at an intermediate stage between fair and gray. His eyes were sharp and quick, formed to take immediate impressions and fix them on paper. His was not a powerful body, though capable enough, and the expression on his wide mouth was one of gentleness. By his trade he must have encountered much that he hated or despised—political chicanery, hypocrisy, opportunism. These would all be basic to the art of the political cartoon in Australia, as they would have been in Britain. But Eve felt that in his personal relationships, his instinct would have been gentle, tolerant, forgiving. There must have been tension between his two sides, unless she was misreading that sunny, accepting face.

"That's enough," he said suddenly. "If you try and get things down in a race with the light, you often ruin the whole picture. It's better to bring it home and try to fix your impressions there." He bent down and began to pack up the canvas bag that had been lying beside his small, collapsible seat.

"You're Steven Coltroon, aren't you," Eve said.

"Steve," he answered automatically. "'You're Steve and like it here. We're a friendly country.' That's one of the national jokes which maybe you haven't heard, young lady. I take it I'm right—you come from 'the old country,' and the northern half of it."

"That's right. I was brought up in Crossley, near Halifax."

"Cr—" He stopped suddenly.

"My name is Eve McNabb."

He had turned to look at her, and now stood up, standing there as if he had just been punched.

"Eve!" he said, with only half his voice. "I've often wondered whether something like this could happen. Dreamed about it, if the truth be known. Come and let me kiss you, love. If I haven't forgotten how to kiss as a father."

She ran to him and he threw his arms around her and held her very close to him as he kissed her, then kissed her again and again. As the third and fourth kiss rained on her, Eve realized that his cheek was wet, then she heard him choking.

"Oh dear, that was good," he said at last. "Let me look at you properly. You're a sight for sore eyes—for old ones too. I always saw you as favoring May, and you do. But I think there's a little bit of me there too."

"I think so too," said Eve. "I found an old snapshot of you at home that gave me some idea, and I thought I could see a lot of me in your face."

"Come along, young lady—by the way, you said you were Eve, didn't you? Not Evelyn."

"Eve."

"I prefer that. We always called you that when you were a baby. But it's Evelyn on your birth certificate, so I thought you might have had the notion of changing how people spoke of you. Lots of young people do. Feel like helping me with my stuff? You can take the easel, I'll take the rucksack. You'll come home with me, won't you? I can find something for dinner, or we can go out for a meal."

"I think I'd like to eat with you, something you like."

"Yes, we've got a lot of catching up to do on little and big things—particularly you, who thought I was dead."

"Oh, you knew that?"

"Yes, May informed me, in a brief note."

"So you kept up communication with each other?" said Eve, very surprised.

"For a short time, occasionally, in staccato sentences."

"I wish she hadn't lied to me."

"Sometimes it's better to, or we think it is. I wonder what I can find in the freezer. And I can make up a bed for you, if you're not fixed up."

"I'm booked into the Ocean View, and I think I'll stick with that. I'll need somewhere I can be alone, collect my impressions, just lie on the bed and think."

"Sure. I understand that. I often need to collect my impressions too. You see some of the politicians here, speaking on television, or deigning to stop here and electioneer, and you think: what is the essence of this shit? Or: how is this old crook developing, which way is he going? And how is my sketch of him going to develop to keep him recognizable and relevant."

"You chose a wonderful profession."

"It chose me. All those people in pubs and places like that—people who looked at me sketching faces and bodies and used to say how good they were. I could have been a pavement artist, and I'd have been happy. But the weather in northern England and Scotland didn't encourage that choice of profession . . . Here we are."

The house was one of the more substantial in a cul-de-sac off the main street, built in brick. Probably it offered more relief from the summer sun than a weatherboard house would have done. It sprawled over a garden of dry grass and the occasional shrub. John McNabb was not a gardener, then, or had had too little time since he became an actual resident here to make a difference. Inside there was substantial old furniture with, in the kitchen, a basic cooker and a large fridge-freezer. Beyond those two rooms there were doors leading to two more, both bedrooms. It all looked simple but comfortable.

"Do I call you John or Steve?" Eve asked as he put together a long concoction of fruit juices. "Dad would come rather unnaturally at first, but I expect I'd get used to it."

"I'd prefer Steve. I'm always called that, and it's what I'm used to. John doesn't exist, but you can call me that in your mind if you like. Dad would seem unnatural to me too: I've never performed the functions of a dad—or not for thirty-odd years."

"And of course I thought you were dead."

"She had her reasons for telling you that, I suppose, and if she decided to do something, that was usually the end of the discussion. I take it she is dead."

"Yes, a couple of weeks ago."

"I assumed that must be the reason for your turning up. May telling you I was alive on her deathbed perhaps."

"No, she never told me."

John McNabb seemed to wish she had. He turned away.

"Of course she probably didn't know about me, one way or the other . . . Now, I wonder what you'd like to eat. Are you a big eater? I was intending to start with prawns—frozen, but straight from the boat to the freezer—then spag Bol, or lasagna or some such thing."

"It sounds ideal."

He went off to the monster fridge-freezer and began rummaging for foil boxes and plastic buckets. Eve noticed there were boxes for two meals as well as for one. Steve had a lot of friends. As he straightened and began to put things together, he threw questions at her.

"So what do you do?"

"I'm in PR. Rather boring and not very useful. I'm thinking of a job change."

"Oh good. What into?"

"Actually, with PR, but much more useful PR."

"Married, with children?"

"Neither. Relationship recently broken up. Hints and possibilities of a future relationship, but nothing definite."

"More promising than the old one then?"

"Much more. Something different, genuine, challenging. Unfortunately, he is married, with a child."

"Does anyone bother themselves with that these days?"

"In the Indian community they do."

"Oh ho-o-o. But I must stop inquisiting you. Tell me about May's death. I'm really sad. She was too young to die."

"Cancer. I was with her at the end."

"Cancer isn't the surefire killer it used to be."

"This one was."

"Was she a good mother? A friend as well as a teacher?"

"Absolutely. I couldn't have been more lucky."

"I knew she would be," said John, with unbounded enthusiasm. "She was a cracker. Even when I married her, when we were both quite young, I knew she was something exceptional."

"So what went wrong then, Steve?"

He came back into the living room and sat down opposite her.

"What does go wrong with early marriages? The obvious things: you regret giving up your freedom, you try regaining it in little ways, and then—"

"Are you thinking of yourself, or Mother?"

"Both, my darling . . . Your mother was a manager, you know."

"Oh, *don't* I know," said Eve, smiling but without rancor.

"She would consult, adapt her ideas in little matters, but in the end she got her own way in ninety-five percent of the things that were being discussed. And all the people involved in the consultation went away thinking she was a wonderful listener and very open to other people's ideas."

"Agreed. I had an advantage because I grew up with

her, I understood her methods, and sometimes I could circumvent them . . . I bet you developed ways of doing that too."

"I'm not sure I did. Maybe I'm just a bit slow. I remember when the job came up in Crossley we discussed it, I said maybe I could do my job just as well away from Glasgow: the McTavish cartoons would not be affected, and the political ones were more often on national matters rather than more parochial Scottish ones. Then one evening we were at a party at the *Tribune* offices and she dragged me over to where she was talking to the proprietor and said it was all settled. I'd be a freelance with special connections to the paper and a commitment to be in Glasgow two days a week." He grimaced. "All miraculously arranged—and without me!"

Eve raised her eyebrows, but not in surprise.

"And did it work?"

"It seemed to at first. I was reveling in being back in Yorkshire, not so far from where I grew up, and where I loved the scenery and the small towns. But there's no substitute for being in the thick of the action. If something important happened—like the three-day week in Heath's premiership—you needed to be *in* your newspaper's office, *with* journalists, in touch with the general reactions of the people who were going to read your paper, you had to judge by their letters, phone calls and so on. Sitting in my home office in 24 Derwent Road, Crossley, trying to judge things through the BBC coverage was nowhere near as good."

"I suppose you resented that?"

"A little. I did try not to. It was an exciting time in other ways because you were born in Crossley, and quite soon after that we bought the house, with help from May's father, and May was enormously enjoying her new job."

"Taking over a lot of the headmistress's work."

"Yes. When May became deputy head, which was quite soon after we arrived. Evelyn made no bones about that, and it suited May, preparing her for what she always wanted: a headship of her own somewhere or other. You can't believe Evelyn Southwell on everything—couldn't, I suppose I should say—but she never hid the fact that she loved teaching and despised administration. You were probably too young to remember her. You were named after her, you know."

"She's still alive, by the way. I met her recently," put in Eve.

"Really? Lucky old Evelyn. She's done better than May. By the way, she and May genuinely liked each other at first, though May would giggle a bit behind her back at her ways and all her little dramas."

"Did the liking cease when Jean Mannering came along?"

"Ah, so you know about her. Yes, that was roughly the turning point. I can't even remember how they met. Some kind of 'do' in Crossley, or Halifax perhaps. Or did May give her a lift in the car?"

"That's what I heard."

"Anyway she clicked immediately with May, who from then on was full of admiration for her—loved her differentness, her sense of adventure, her love of saying and doing outrageous things."

"Jean was much younger than May, wasn't she?"

"Yes, by several years. But even so, somehow, she always seemed to be the leader."

"Were you jealous?"

John shifted in his chair and frowned.

"Common sense suggests that I probably was. Certainly I *became* jealous. But in the early stages, as I remember it, I was mostly amused. You know Jean was a lesbian? I knew May was not lesbian, though she found the *idea* of it attractive. I also knew that behind Evelyn Southwell's relationship with May there was a strong lesbian impulse."

"*Evelyn's?*"

"Oh yes. Didn't you get it? You say you've met her."

"Oh yes. We've talked."

"Well, maybe the fires have burned themselves low by now. But look at the situation: May is a new teacher in a new school, and almost at once she gets loaded with administrative work that was not just donkey work but often quite important stuff. The fact that she did it brilliantly, the fact that everyone recognized May as future headmistress material, are neither here nor there. The fact is, the situation was very unusual, could have aroused real jealousy, and was sometimes downright irregular. It was favoritism of the usual kind, based on sex. Evelyn wanted her favorite to be recognized as a star. Evelyn fancied her rotten, though it was in the balance whether she would risk her position, and May's, by proposing any physical relationship."

"Which way did the balance go?"

"Toward 'no.' But that may be because Jean had come into the picture."

Eve thought for a time, and in the silence John slipped out and brought in prawns.

"Evelyn said she ditched her husband because she couldn't bear him near her," said Eve. "And she was very scathing about how May's work went downhill as soon as she got involved with Jean."

"*That* was a downright lie," said John, popping a prawn into his mouth. "I know that. People were always full of praise for the way May did her double job. That's how I knew the job would always come first—was the thing she prized most. That hurt, perhaps more than the business with Jean."

"You thought that the job came before her marriage?"

John pondered this.

"Well, it wasn't quite like that. But after a year or two in Crossley, the marriage wasn't going well. May was getting her most pleasurable hours with Jean, not with me. I was getting mine with you. It was a rotten situation. The basis of the marriage was crumbling under our feet."

As John changed their plates and doled out spaghetti and sauce, Eve thought about the situation in the house, which she now lived in, or camped in, when she was hardly more than a baby.

"Jean says there was never a physical relationship between them," she said as they settled down over their food. John pulled a face.

"I suspect she was lying. So you've talked to her too? What's she like now?"

"Not quite the original and energetic soul everyone paints her as when they talk about her thirty years ago. But then, who is? She's got into religion, by the way."

"Really? Well, that I never would have suspected. But religion gets a hold on the most curious people. Rupert Murdoch, for example . . . I suspected at the time that they did sleep together but that May found it—how shall I put it?—irrelevant, neither exciting nor disgusting but beside the point. She was interested in the friendship, that was where the life and the vigor of the relationship lay. In any case it's pretty irrelevant now. The important point is that Jean was young, hot and very determined. She realized that as long as May remained a teacher, particularly in a small Yorkshire town, there was no question of an open relationship. But she was determined, if she could, to destroy May's and my marriage, to make herself the central, dominant figure in May's life and to gain the nearest thing possible to the open relationship she craved. Me out of the way, and of course with the child, you, remaining with the mother, as went without saying then— it was to be the perfect little family group, from her point of view."

Eve meditated on the picture. It seemed to make sense, though perhaps more with the young Jean of popular report than with the older Jean she had met. Perhaps religion had wrought change.

"So how did she take May along with her?" she asked. "I don't believe my mother would go along with anything underhand or crooked."

"May didn't know. That's the whole point of the story: the biter bit. When May found out what Jean had done, she assured me she was utterly shocked. She broke with Jean forever."

"Yes, I heard that, though Jean assured me it was just

a natural wastage of friendship over time. So what did Jean do? This was on the weekend when you and May were both away, separately, wasn't it?"

"Yes. I went straight to Glasgow as usual early Wednesday morning, leaving a note for May with my London hotel's phone number on it. After my usual two days, which was in fact a day and a half there, I flew down to London. The reason I went there was that I had been offered an interview with the editor of the *Observer*."

"A job interview? As their cartoonist?"

"No, just an interview. I'd approached them, they were responding. Perhaps they were just being kind. When I had the interview, on Friday, early evening, the editor said they could be interested long term, at some time in the future. But he felt my recent stuff had lost a lot of the punch and energy of the earlier work I did for the *Tribune*. It was exactly what I thought myself, but depressing to hear it from someone else. It was a helpful interview though, it set me thinking how I'd lost a lot of the brio of my earlier political stuff. Was this a normal stage of growing up? Was I getting stale? Or was I just out of things, away from the action? I tried to ring May, who was in Birmingham, but she wasn't in the hotel room. I never managed to contact her that evening."

"So what happened?"

"I got a phone call in my hotel room. I'd had a couple of drinks, but any fuzziness cleared the moment I heard the voice. It was Jean Mannering. I thought, Watch it!"

"Why?"

"She'd been encroaching for months. Making decisions about Eve—sorry, you, my dear—getting the keys to the house, making unusual calls on May (calls she usually resisted, I may say). Now she started off: 'Listen very carefully, John. You're going to have to make a big decision.'"

"She sounds as if she was power crazed."

"Do you think so? I don't think she was ever crazed. She went on: 'You must know by now, John, that your marriage with May is over. She's bored, you're in a rut. Did the *Observer* offer you a job today, by the way?' 'No, they didn't.' 'You see? You're in a rut. You need a great big change in your life. Here's the offer. If you go to Heathrow early tomorrow morning, you'll find waiting for you a single ticket to Australia, all paid for.' I just laughed and said: 'Manna from heaven! What if I said "I'd rather die?"' She said: 'In effect, you have no choice. I know you *can* go. You have your passport.' That was in my note to May. She had started to annoy me. 'Is this some conspiracy with May?' I demanded. Because we'd discussed the need for a warmer climate, and I'd told her I might take off for a month or two to Majorca. I didn't like the thought of Jean reading my notes to May, but I liked the idea of my future being discussed between them even less. 'No, it isn't,' said Jean. 'But I'm sure she'd sympathize.' I blew up: 'May is much too sensible to sympathize with nonsense like this. And bullying like this. We'll solve our problems in our own way and time.' And then it came out."

"What?"

"The clincher. The reason I had no choice. Jean said: 'If you don't get on that plane, the ten thirty BA flight 674 to Sydney, the police will be informed that in your house there is a rich collection of explicit pornography involving underage girls.'"

Eve stared at him.

"But I don't understand. Why—"

"I said: 'There is no such collection,' and Jean said: 'There is now.'"

"She'd put a collection of pornography in the house?"

"Oh yes. You can see how she could have got hold of one. One branch of lesbian taste and one branch of male hetero taste for once coinciding."

"But it wouldn't have your fingerprints on it."

"In a way absence of fingerprints would be as suspicious as the presence of them. It would show that I knew what I was doing was illegal. And of course it still is. People caught downloading such stuff from the Internet get caught routinely and jailed for quite long periods."

"But I still don't see—"

"Think about it. Jean was trading on the fact of my tenderness for May and my pride in her achievements. Where would her career as a primary school highflier be if her husband was arrested for possessing explicit pornography involving little girls? Even continuing to employ her would involve terrible publicity and an orchestrated public outcry from parents and an orgy of righteousness from the tabloids. My career would be in tatters, especially if I was jailed. That cartoonist with the series about the McTavishes. Just a dirty old man at heart. And with *children*! Little girls! London in the seventies may still have been swinging, but I can tell you Glasgow was much less swinging, and Edinburgh never swung at all, except at festival time, rather genteelly. Oh, she was clever, was Jean. She chose just the right thing that would ruin both May and me."

"I'm beginning to see. So what did you do?"

"I hemmed and hawed, I accused her of all sorts of things (with good reason and good evidence), but in the end, as she said, there was no choice. I said 'I'll be on that plane,' and next morning I was, with what I stood up in, a change of underwear and shirt, and that was about it. I knew our marriage was crumbling anyway, and I couldn't ruin May's career to keep it going for a few months. We had no future. The fact that May had brought our marriage to the brink of disaster by associating with a ruthless little pirate like Jean only made me more convinced I had to move on. Leaving you was the hardest thing of all, but I couldn't stay with you without ruining May and myself. Next morning I got the first underground train to Heathrow, collected my ticket and got on the plane."

"Do you think you were watched?"

"I don't know. I didn't even think about it. Maybe Jean knew someone at Heathrow. Maybe she got in her car—alone or with a friend—and went down to keep watch herself and make sure I got on. It would be like her: she loved action, the chase, doing unusual things herself."

"Why do you mention a friend?"

"Because all the time during the phone call, I could hear voices in the background, and all of them were women's voices. I wondered if she was ringing from the club for lesbians that met in Halifax every Friday. Sapphonics, they called it. But I've no reason to think she had an accomplice."

"One thing: you mention Jean possibly driving down herself. She and May met when May offered her a lift. What was Jean doing by the time your marriage split up?"

"Oh, she'd left the tax office and gone into business— got a nice little job with a textile firm, a well-paid job. She had a little sports car, bright red and zippy."

"And now she's gone into the church. I wish I could understand Jean."

"I wish I'd understood her, back then. I must say that if she's gone into the church in the sense I think you mean, the Church of England has changed a hell of a lot since I lived in England."

John cleared away the plates, and they by tacit agreement changed the subject. They talked about Australia, how he had come to love it, how his style of cartooning had changed, how the jokes had become more vitriolic as he had come to hate Australian politicians, how the sacking of Gough Whitlam soon after he arrived had made his name as a political cartoonist and he had never looked back. He was enormously chuffed that Eve had seen and liked his initial reaction to the sacking.

"To think it's led you to me! . . . But I always did love a political earthquake. Even now, when a new scandal is brewing, my cartoon finger starts itching and soon some newspaper or other phones me up and offers me nice little sums to return to the fray."

"And you do," said Eve.

"Yes, I do. I can't resist."

Later he and Eve walked back to the Ocean View, and he kissed her on the step of her room. She felt unusually happy, and was sure her body told her that he was happy too, that a change had come over his life, in its last phase, that was infinitely to his taste.

Going to bed, Eve had a sense of having been made whole.

CHAPTER 11

Four Score and Five

The rest of the week was for Eve a time of the sharpest pleasures she thought she had ever known. First she was shown the coast by one who knew it better, in more closely observed detail, than most natives of the area knew it. Then they drove—Eve drove—down to Sydney, and she was shown, again, things that only an artist—sometimes only a satirical artist—would know about and appreciate. The spring sun was warm, the occasional breeze was welcome, and the days passed in happiness, community of tastes, and endless new experiences in food, in animals and vegetation, in people and their habits and assumptions. John was showing off his Australianness.

"You must come again, and properly," said John. "And bring your Indian boyfriend."

"I'm not sure he could get away. Policemen always seem to get their leave canceled at the last moment. Anyway, would he be allowed in?"

"If he's got a British passport, he shouldn't have any difficulty."

Eve screwed up her face.

"Imagine the awfulness of making the flight, being turned away by immigration, then having to do it backward."

"It wouldn't happen. Anyway you could make damned sure in advance that it *wasn't* going to happen."

"You're ignoring the fact that planes fly in the other direction. Have you never had an urge to see the places that you knew again?"

John shook his head violently.

"I can honestly say no. Or not since the early months out here. To tell you the truth, it was the last months back there that made me ready for a completely new start, and that's what happened. I've never wanted to retrace my steps."

"It's not the police, is it? Surely once you were out of the country, Jean would have retrieved the pornography and the police would never have been involved."

"No, it's not the police. It's nothing about England. It's about me."

The subject of John's departure from England and Eve's life there came up now and then, but casually, a matter of detail, rather than anything central or vital. One time when they were talking about the McNabbs' early years in Crossley, Eve asked John who would know most about them.

"Is George Wilson still alive? May's colleague at the school?" he asked.

"Yes, he was at the funeral."

"Have you talked to him?"

"A bit."

LAST POST

"Try again. He's not a gossip by nature, but he's quiet and trustworthy and he gets told things. He was devoted to your mother, and he might be willing to pass on what he knows to you. It's worth a try."

Another time, Eve never could remember how, the subject of Jean Mannering's family background came up.

"Her parents kept the general store in Crossley. I suppose these days you'd call it a corner shop."

"These days there isn't such a thing in Crossley. Everyone goes to the supermarket two miles out of the village."

"Anyway, they more or less showed Jean the door."

"Like the Menzies figure in your cartoon?"

"Not quite. There was no illegitimate child, of course, and they didn't say they never wanted to see her again. They just said they didn't want her living there. People criticized them a lot about that. Rumors were going around about Jean's sexual tastes, and some of the more liberal minded said they were punishing her for being lesbian. I don't think it was that at all."

"What do you think it was?"

"I think the Mannerings were fed up with being organized, told what to do, dragooned into doing it. Jean was incurably bossy. More bossy than May. Give her a friend, show her a colleague, and Jean would turn them into underlings. Maybe she's changed, but I doubt she could."

"She may have got more subtle about it," said Eve. "I didn't sense a bossiness."

"Yes, sometimes people do get more subtle with age. But it's the means that change, not the ends."

In between sightseeing they visited the offices of the *Australian Guardian,* several drinking holes frequented by

167

journos, and they ate well at John's favorite restaurants and bars. Everywhere he found friends, and Eve wondered at the way he had Australianized himself in everything except his accent. He seemed to have an encyclopedic knowledge of every sordid little deal or quid pro quo that national and state politicians kept well hidden from the general public. "He owes him one" was his favorite summing up of the relationship between two typical party politicos. Eve thought she was getting a brilliant overview of the underbelly of Australian statecraft.

On the night before she flew home, they arrived at the hotel to find the receptionist had attached a message to Eve's room key. She looked at John and raised an eyebrow. She detached the paper and looked at it:

> Evelyn Southwell found dead. Can't wait to see you. OMKAR.

"Well," said her father, "I said she'd done a lot better than May. The old sinner should be grateful for all those extra years."

"I think there might be more to it than that, Dad. Omkar says 'found dead.' I think he was trying to tell me something without being too explicit."

Whether or not the receptionist had registered the "found dead" she certainly had noted "Dad." Till then she had put them down as lovers ill-matched in age. Eve only remembered what she had said when she was having a long bath in her room. Saying the word so naturally, without premeditation, pleased her. She was awarding John his place in her life. She was also staking a claim in his.

She had plenty of time to meditate on this the next day, when she caught her plane from Sydney and settled back into the attitude of cogitation that had been so difficult on her way out. Now at least she had two new subjects for meditation, and that of her father and the late establishment of links between them gave her unlimited satisfaction. In fact, she decided, happiness would be a better word. She believed he was a generous and civilized man, and even if he had not been her father, she would have been happy and proud to be his friend.

Then there was Evelyn Southwell. Her death certainly bore thinking about. She felt quite certain that if, say, she had died after a stroke, Rani would not have bothered to send her a telephone message. She decided she ought to get her thoughts in order. First she remembered back to their interview, and after she had focused on two or three things she recalled of the encounter, things Evelyn had said, she thought she had better be more ordered. She got out a notebook and pen and set down what she remembered, the subjects they had covered and the sequence in which they were discussed. Then she noted any memorable things that Evelyn had said. By the time she had finished, she felt she had the entire conversation fixed in her mind.

Then, after some thought, she added some notes on the subsequent conversation with Jean Mannering.

Why, she wondered, if there was anything suspect about Evelyn Southwell's death, did she instinctively consider the possibility that Jean Mannering had anything to do with it? The only answer she could come up with was that years ago—three decades and more ago—the two women had apparently been in conflict over her mother.

And her mother, apparently, had not been attracted to either Jean or Evelyn in the way they had wanted her to be attracted. It was odd, but Eve had no evidence that Evelyn and Jean had ever done more than have brief encounters with each other. She seemed to be straying into the realm of, at least, the far-fetched.

Eve herself felt more dead than alive when at last, after two rotten films, several meals of tasteless food, insipid conversation and *The Four Seasons* on the music channel, they arrived at Manchester Airport. In so far as her spirits could rise at all they rose at the sight of Omkar waiting with a small knot of other people at the exit from customs. They kissed with all the enthusiasm Eve could muster and Omkar took her case.

"I did a double shift yesterday," he said as they walked toward the car park. "It was sheer extortion on my part because in the second shift I was only thinking in bottom gear. But it means a colleague is standing in for me today."

"Your meeting me is a wonderful service. I couldn't ask for better. Excuse me if I give the impression of being half dead. It's because I am."

"Oh, I know the effects of journeys from Australia. I've had to meet people who were extradited and they've never been fit for questioning for forty-eight hours after they get back. You can go to sleep in the car."

"It seems so ungrateful."

"Much better than us trying to make conversation and you feeling like death the whole time. But before you doze off, I'll tell you about Mrs. Southwell."

"Please. At least that will prove I'm not a suspect. I gather you think she was murdered?"

"Yes, and you, my dear, were ten thousand miles away. As we proved by ringing your hotel."

So as they drove through Southport, Omkar told her about the death.

"I expect you remember the setup at Autumn Prospect, don't you?"

"Pretty much. Roughly three sides of a square, with all the flats having a view of the central square, and some over the wall to the road beyond, because the square is on a slope. The flats are grouped into five or six, and each group is cut off from the rest, and has its own door from the outside. This is probably to prevent it feeling like a jail or a boarding school. So each flat opens on to a corridor, but the corridor is blocked off at both ends to make the flats into a separate unit."

"Very good," said Rani approvingly. "So ideally any intruder would need keys to the appropriate door into the corridor, then one into the flat. One maid does the cleaning for one group of flats. Mrs. Southwell was found in the morning by the maid."

"Was there only one cleaner's visit a day?"

"If there was no reason for more. There are degrees of incapacity there. Also there is a night caretaker nurse who sees that everything is all right, and answers calls. Mrs. Southwell's light was on at ten o'clock, which is unusual, and the caretaker went in to switch it off. She says Mrs. Southwell was alive and well then so far as she could tell. She was asleep, noisily."

"You sound dubious. Is she reliable?"

"Reliable, but not the most capable of the staff there. The manager admitted that. But on the whole we believe her. She is very insistent that she saw the face clearly, and there were no signs of lividity then."

"So she was killed—if she was—by an intruder at some time after ten?"

"Yes. It would not be difficult to get in during the evening because the porter potters around and answers calls, of which there were usually several, often old people just wanting a talk, or to air a grievance or to rake over a quarrel with one of the other inmates. He does a bit of inspection before locking the gate sometime around eleven. There's a notice up to this effect on the door. He dozes or reads through the night—he has to be reasonably alert, because there are sometimes emergencies."

"So between ten and eleven seems indicated?"

"Roughly. Right, I think that's all you can take in for the moment. Anyway I just wanted to tell you the uncontested facts. I'll leave the rest to someone higher up in the investigation. Now you go to sleep."

And she did, and only awoke when Omkar shook her as they approached Crossley. As he kissed her good night at the front door and heaved her suitcase into the hallway, he said:

"Superintendent Collins wants to talk to you. I said you wouldn't be human until Monday morning. Is that right?"

"At the moment I can't imagine ever being human again. But yes—that's right."

She was on her way up to bed before she realized that she had not asked Omkar about himself and his situation.

But then, for most of the journey from the airport, she had been asleep. She slept for twelve hours, and when she awoke she rather surprisingly remembered Omkar's remarks of the day before about Superintendent Collins. It was Saturday, but she rang his office and made an appointment for Monday. Then she washed her hair, shopped for fresh supplies of basics, had another long sleep, somehow got through the English Sunday, sacred to consumerism, and, through all this, put her thoughts in order for the next day.

Collins made it clear from the beginning of the interview that he wanted to talk about the case. He mentioned her visit to the victim, went on to detail the events of Evelyn Southwell's last day, and the arrangements at Autumn Prospect.

"From a security point of view, they were all haywire. One could imagine a confused old resident getting out of the place and going walkabout without any difficulty. But Autumn Prospect doesn't cater to that sort of elderly person—they find them a place in a nursing home when it gets to that stage. And you can't blame them for not envisaging that a murderer will get in, kill one of the residents there and then walk nonchalantly out. That's what seems to have happened."

"So I gathered from Rani's account. And perhaps there was an earlier visit too, to secure somehow the keys to Mrs. Southwell's room?"

Collins's face expressed uncertainty.

"Certainly there's no sign of a break-in. On the other hand, the locks are simple Yale ones, at least the ones to the rooms are, with the usual simple locking device that can be slipped down on the inside, in other words by the old person, who may be feeling unsafe."

"Not really adequate, I'd have thought," said Eve.

"Security in places for old people is difficult: by definition they are closer to death than most, and staff need to be able to get to them easily in an emergency. But yes, we do think that somehow the key to Mrs. Southwell's door had been obtained by the killer."

"There is no doubt that it's murder?"

"None now. We have the pathologist's report. We'll be announcing it to the media tonight. Suffocation is not something that's easy to be sure of, but the signs were pretty conclusive."

"So what do you want from me?"

"First of all background to the victim. Who was she, what had she done in her lifetime, what was she like. I knew her once as a head teacher. What was she like as a woman? Start with Mr. Southwell."

Eve thought for some time.

"Mr. Southwell is probably not worth worrying about. Very short marriage early in life, dismissed as a mistake. Come back to that later. She was a teacher, as you know, and spent her working life in educational establishments. She was—you know all this, but I'll say it for the record—my mother's headmistress when she became teacher then deputy head at Blackfield Road. Evelyn Southwell later went on to be head of a school in Bradford. She seems to have been a good teacher, but as you remember she was showy, one who impressed her personality on children—

rather a dated concept now, but I'd say it's one way of being a good teacher."

"Right. Now what about her personality?"

Eve, looking at his determined, downright face, thought he was quite as likely to have an opinion as she did.

"Egotistical," she said. "A performer. Went through life thinking only of herself, though she could become fond of people, as she did of my mother. And by the way, coming back to her marriage: it could be that the reason why this was a mistake was that Evelyn had lesbian tendencies."

Collins raised his eyebrows.

"Oh? Who suggests this?"

"My father. You know I've just been to Australia to see him? Okay, he could be biased, but he had good reasons to give, and they convinced me. So there could have been a sort of genteel battle for my mother's affections. A battle which Evelyn lost."

"Interesting. But a long time ago. A long, long time."

"Yes. It's difficult to be sure it's relevant."

"On the other hand, it could offer a pointer to more recent things that might be relevant."

"Oh, and by the way, after I'd visited her and spoken about the past, I rang up Jean Mannering to put her in the picture."

"I see. Rani has told me about her. Why did you do that?"

"I wanted to be clear in my mind about how much Jean would admit to knowing about my father's—let's call it *disappearance* to Australia, because that's what it virtually was. Now, having talked to him about it, I can say pretty definitely that Jean was lying."

"I see. And the truth?"

"That Jean was the prime mover in his going there, a rather subtle form of blackmail."

"Right. Let's come back to that later. Can you give me the gist of your conversation with Mrs. Southwell—all the way through?"

"Yes. I've gone over this in my mind and made a few notes." She took them from her handbag. "We began with the courtesies. Evelyn revealed that she thought I'd gone to Blackfield and been one of her pupils. I think she subconsciously assumed this so that she could talk about herself rather than my mother, who I'd told her I wanted to talk about. I didn't put her right about the school, but I did make it clear I wanted to talk about my mother. And my father."

"What was her reaction to your mentioning your father?"

"Vague. She clearly didn't know him well, or have any feelings for or against him. But she went along with my idea that he might not be dead. Going through what she said and how she said it, I think it's unlikely she was involved in the plot to get him out of the country, and out of the marriage, but I think we should leave open the possibility that she knew about it."

"Point taken."

"We got on to why my mother would lie about his death and that led the conversation on to sex. She was rather disappointed when I mentioned Jean Mannering.

She wanted to surprise me on that subject, and she found I'd already met Jean and had some ideas of my own."

"She didn't mention any competition with Jean for your mother's affections?"

"No, certainly not. We didn't talk about her sexual orientation at all. She just said that after meeting Jean my mother became erratic and unreliable, which my father says is untrue. She also mentioned that Jean landed up in the Church of England, which she seems to regard as a proof of eccentricity."

"Dear, dear. Though eccentricity does sometimes come as a result," said Collins, grinning.

"I'm rather out on a limb where religion is concerned. I wasn't brought up to have one, merely to conform when necessary. Anyway we talked about whether there was an affair between Jean and my mother—she thought not, but thought the friendship was destroying my parents' marriage. Then she mentioned my father's taking off to Australia, which she thought might be due to Jean Mannering: she used the word 'trick,' which was close enough to what actually happened to make me think she knew a lot about it."

"Your mother could have told her."

"I don't think that was likely at that stage in the relationship."

"Maybe not. What about your mother and Jean after your father disappeared?"

"It was the end of their closeness. Absolutely the end. I think what was done was so bad, so outside the limits to my mother that she wanted nothing more to do with Jean."

"Can you tell me what was done?"

"I think so. It's a long time ago, and my father says he's never coming back to this country. Jean got together a stack of child pornography involving young girls and put it into my parents' house after they had both gone off—May to Birmingham, John to Glasgow and London. Jean rang him at his London hotel, said there was a one-way air ticket to Australia waiting for him at Heathrow, and threatened that if he didn't take the plane the next morning, the police would be called in, alerted to the porn."

Superintendent Collins took some time to think this over.

"Neat. It could have been the deathblow to his wife's career, as well as his own."

"Exactly. And Jean was supposed to be in love with my mother. I can't work out whether she would have carried out her threat or not."

"If I was him I'd have brazened it out."

"But what Jean knew was that the marriage was close to being on the rocks, though my dad still had a lot of love and respect for Mum and love for me. I think he half-welcomed the chance to escape from all the emotional mess, though I don't suppose he liked the tail-between-the-legs aspect of the whole business."

"It says a lot for Jean Mannering's nerve and cheek, that's for sure."

"That's what I think. And my guess is that Evelyn was, in a way, jealous of that in-your-face daring."

"How would you sum up Evelyn's attitude during the talk you had with her?"

"I think she was playing with me," said Eve promptly. "I think initially she welcomed the attention—*any* attention was sweet, I suspect—but got annoyed by the fact that I already knew a lot of what she was going to hint at or tantalize me with. I would guess that if she had lived she would have called me back and started dribbling out further bits of information, claiming she had 'just remembered' them, or not told me out of consideration for Jean or my mother's memory."

"All very interesting. And when you talked to Jean Mannering afterward?"

"I think I may have let slip, just from my tone of voice, that I didn't necessarily believe her account of the vital weekend. And I certainly talked about the possibility of Evelyn coming up with more 'revelations.'" Eve decided to be frank. "I wish I hadn't now. I have to face the possibility that—"

Collins put up his hand.

"Don't stray into the realms of distant possibility, and don't blame yourself. The person to blame for murder is the murderer. We can none of us foresee every remote possibility of consequences for our actions." He stood up. "I'm sure you'll understand that on the other matter we talked about, we can't proceed any further at the moment—not till the matter of Mrs. Southwell is cleared up."

"Oh, I hadn't thought about that. No, of course you can't. Even though I was in Australia at the time."

"We know that, and have checked. That's not really in question, but you could be a vital witness, and giving you a job while the investigation is ongoing—well, all things considered, we'd better wait."

"And I should put on hold any inquiries I've been making?"

"I can't see that we can have any objection to investigation by you of your mother's early life. If anything comes up about that, you have the best possible contact with us. But Rani won't talk to you about the investigation we're conducting, and I'm sure you won't try to get anything out of him."

"No, of course not. On the whole I think it's thoroughly healthy if he and I try to talk exclusively of other things."

Eve tried to follow her own resolution on the journey home, and as she threw together a few things for a meal. She tried to think about her future life, about whether, if she got the job with the West Yorkshire Police Headquarters, it would provide the sort of change she ought to be aiming for. On the whole she thought it would. On the other hand, she would be working with Rani, even if he was very low down in the chain of responsibility there. If things didn't work out between them, this could prove to be a negative aspect. Except that she couldn't think of Rani in terms of a thorn in the flesh, or of ever being on bad terms with him.

She was thinking about him, as she very often did, when the front doorbell went. It was what she was beginning to think of as his ring—a firm ring lasting for about a second. When she opened the door, he was standing there in open-necked shirt, jeans and with his jacket over his shoulder.

"Rani! Come in. I've just had supper, but I can put something together for you."

"I'm not hungry." His voice shook with uncertainty. "I won't come in till you've said yes to me."

"That sounds like blackmail."

"There is only one thing I want you to do for me. I want you to come to bed with me and make love all night."

He had hardly finished the sentence before she said "Yes! Oh, yes please!" and threw herself on him and kissed him in the well-lit porch of the house. Then she dragged him inside.

CHAPTER 12

The Intruder

Eve lay in bed, watching Omkar dress. She felt a happiness that she did not think it was possible to put into words. She had thought she was happy with her father in Sydney, but that was nothing to this—nothing like this. But as he slipped on his shirt and looked around for his jacket, the words suddenly came to her.

"I love you so much."

He looked around and smiled—a happy but somehow shy smile. He came and kissed her good-bye on the forehead.

"I thought you were still asleep."

"I was pretending to be, for the pleasure of watching you. In the end the words just came out. Simple but true."

"Simple is best."

"Why did you come to me last night?"

"Because I wanted to, and at last I could. Sanjula has left what we call 'the family home.' Taken my beautiful daughter, but I faced up to that before it happened. I shall see her often—they are remaining in this country. We have started the divorce action, and she will marry a boy of her own age from her home village in India. I feel like the weight of the world has been lifted from my shoulders . . . What are you going to do today?"

"Walk around hugging myself at my unbelievable good fortune. Oh, and there is someone, an old teacher of my mother's generation, who I might try to have a talk with, if I can come down from cloud nine and get my feet firmly on the ground."

"Until next time."

"Definitely until next time. What are you going to do?"

"That depends on Superintendent Collins. I think he is probably going to send us to scout around Autumn Prospect."

"Sorry, I shouldn't have asked that. Collins emphasized that your lips are to be sealed on the subject of the investigation."

Rani grinned.

"A bit late for that. We seem to have talked it over a hell of a lot already."

"Well, you'd better get the lip glue. The last thing I'd want is to be any hindrance to your career with the police. Though now I come to think about it, most of our talk was before it became a case."

"Don't think too much about it. Treat it as one of those ritual warnings that people seem bound to give in all sorts of situations these days."

"That's for fear of future lawsuits. I will try to be careful. I could so easily let slip something that only you could have told me."

"Don't lose sleep over it. And who knows? This could be a case that is solved almost before it becomes a case. A lot of murders are like that, though you wouldn't think so from watching the television." He came back and kissed her. "I love you so much," he said. "I finish at four. Shall we meet up then?" It was a question that hardly needed an answer.

Eve lived the first part of the morning in an ecstatic dream. Everything in the house and garden seemed to have taken on a new shine, gained a deeper interest for her. Was this where she was again going to live? She had no doubt that they could. She wished Omkar had told her more about what happened at the end of his old life, the married life. He had been in a hurry, but she had no doubt he wanted, perhaps subconsciously, to say as little about it as possible. And she wanted to avoid the appearance of pressuring him. She too felt the impulse to live for and enjoy the moment, to avoid looking at any problems or drawbacks fair and square. Reality would come, probably in the shape of Omkar's parents. But why hasten the process?

About half-past eleven she looked up George Wilson in the telephone directory, then put on walking shoes and made her way through the village. She hoped that her inner feelings of ecstasy did not make themselves too plain on her face. George was living in a large bungalow with neat paths and beds, and he greeted her cheerfully.

"George, are you busy?"

"I'm never busy. I'm a retired old schoolteacher. I'm also a widower, which means there are plenty of things I can either do or leave undone. Mostly I'm happy to leave them undone. Dusting and hoovering are options, not imperatives. Who'd bother themselves winning brownie points from the dead? What have you in mind?"

"A pub lunch, on me. Is there anywhere in the village that does a good one?"

"Oh, the Speckled Cow does a very acceptable one, if you're not after anything fussy. But I suppose you've gone over entirely to Indian food now, have you?"

Eve's eyes narrowed, but she was not nonplussed.

"That was unworthy of you, George. But it at least means your snouts are keeping you well informed."

"You're getting the police jargon already. I hope you're grateful. So far as I can see, you owe it all to me."

"I am and I do."

"I'll just get my jacket and we'll be on our way."

The Speckled Cow was only five minutes away, and they ordered gammon and chips, Timothy Taylor's Landlord bitter and an orange squash, then looked for a table. The Cow, at just after twelve on a weekday, was not bustling with activity, and they found a distant table where they could be alone.

"It's information I want," said Eve.

"Of course it is, my dear. And how was Australia?"

She shot him a quick glance.

"Hmmm. I suppose all business in Crossley is anyone's business. Well, it was pretty much like it looks in the soaps. And my father is alive, was delighted to see me, and if I'd known him all my life, I suspect I would love him as girls mostly do love their fathers."

"And did he tell you why he left—but I mustn't pry . . ."

He busied himself with his pipe, but a sharp eye was looking at her. Eve shook her head.

"And you wouldn't get anywhere if you did. I suppose you heard about Evelyn Southwell's death?"

"I did. And I heard the announcement last night that there were suspicious circumstances. I must admit I was surprised."

"Oh? Why?"

"I think with any murder—if that's what it was—you look at the character and circumstances of the victim, don't you? To get to the *why*? And I can't see any *why* in the case of old Southwell. Oh, she was showy, prickly, faintly ridiculous, and nobody was important in her world except herself. But if you killed off all the prickly and self-important people working in our schools, there'd be a severe teacher shortage. And besides, she'd been retired for twenty-odd years. What could there be about her that provoked murder after all these years of blameless retirement?"

"Good point. George, when we talked at the funeral, you didn't mention the name of Jean Mannering."

George Wilson screwed up his face.

"Ah! Well, why would I? You may remember I wasn't particularly keen on the idea of you raking up your mother's past."

"I remember very well."

"But of course that didn't stop you. Has it brought you happiness?"

"It's brought me a great many things, including a father."

"So we've said, and I'm glad you're grateful."

"But so far as my mother was concerned, I wasn't looking for happiness. I was looking for . . . well, let's call it enlightenment. And I think I'm getting it, gradually. But you haven't answered my question."

Their food arrived. The gammon was dry and the chips half cold. George Wilson tucked in with relish, and Eve answered "lovely" to his inquiries. Her mother had told her that the truth should always be told except on social occasions, when lies are better than embarrassment for all. Looking over her mother's life Eve felt that, like most parents, May had not always lived up to her own precepts.

"Well?"

"Of course we knew about Jean Mannering, all those of us on the staff at Blackfield Road. And we said at the time—or rather *speculated*—in the same vein as everyone else: were they lovers, and so on. After all, we were teachers. We may not have been masterminds, but we weren't weakest links either. We had rough ideas about a whole range of sexual preferences; we knew, or thought we did, about the Sapphonics club in Halifax, so we thought we knew all about Jean Mannering and where *her* tastes lay. And this was a village, where nearly everyone knew nearly everyone else. We didn't *know* if what was going on was an affair. Why would May have a lesbian affair when she was, so far as we knew, a happily married young woman with a new baby who made both her parents very happy."

"So the general feeling was that there was no affair?"

"Ye-e-es. General but not universal. What opinion is?"

"And what did the other opinion say?"

"That John and your mother had been married quite a

long time, that she—and, for that matter, he—could be bored, that they were relieving the boredom by trying out new things. They were, in fact, several years late for the seven-year-itch, which came up rather often in the conversations."

"I must say I hadn't thought of that. So Jean was notorious at least by village standards?"

"Pretty much so. When the friendship with May broke up, there was another almost immediately, and that *was* an affair, no question."

"Right . . ." She thought for a moment. "Would you say you had followed Jean's life?"

"No. How could I, with her and her parents both moved away from the village? I've followed what I've read in the paper, which would be her public life. And I've heard village gossip, which I certainly never assume to be reliable. And in any case, since her parents moved away and there was nobody else to ask about her, there hasn't been the same interest in her."

"They moved a fair way away?"

"Down to be near their son in Peterborough."

"Tell me what you know about her public life."

George thought and ate on, with enjoyment. His standards had probably slipped since he'd become a widower.

"It's been an odd life. Directionless—or rather, with too many directions. Or perhaps the point has been the relationships, and I don't know much about those except in general. She was working in the local tax office when she and May met, but she soon moved into local industry—there was still a textile industry then—and of course she wasn't on the factory floor, she was at managerial level. It was quite an innovation at that time, appointing a woman to an important job in industry. People talked about it a lot, and plenty of them shook their heads. It wasn't the sort of thing people around here liked."

"Was it successful? My father says she was bossy by nature and turned everybody into underlings."

"Did he say that?" He put his knife and fork back on his plate and looked ahead of him. "You know, it's like hearing someone from the dead, you quoting him like that. He was quite right, but that didn't make her unsuccessful. Quite the reverse. You might say northerners are used to little Hitlers—the inheritance of the industrial revolution, when factory owners—the bad ones—were little better than slave drivers. So once they got used to a woman boss, things went well, and Jean got results while she worked in Halifax, though she couldn't buck the national trend: textiles were a declining industry, in fact a doomed one."

"What about spare-time activities? I know she was an amateur actress."

"Oh yes, for quite a while. Very good too, it's said, took on big parts and did them well. Don't suppose there were the same opportunities in London—too big and busy, and too much professional competition for the little amateur drama groups to thrive."

"I suppose so. But when was she in London?"

That needed consideration. Still, George was good on time.

"I'd say some time in the eighties. About six or seven

years she was away from the Yorkshire area. Mid-eighties, I'd say."

"But she came back?"

"She did that. Maybe they didn't respond so well to her methods in the south. Maybe the competition was too fierce in London. She was an executive in a chain of women's shops, specializing in the teenage and young twenties market. When she came back she said she was tired of London—of course she did, they all do—and that she had had an offer she couldn't refuse, and loved being back in Yorkshire."

"You're sounding cynical, George."

"Offers you can't refuse tend to be angled for before they get made. She was unhappy in London, people think, and not doing as well as expected there. She got out before she was pushed."

"So she came back here, did more drama—oh, what was the job, by the way?"

"She was part of the management team for Woolworth's, in West Yorkshire."

"Right. More money than the first job in textiles, but maybe not more interesting."

"Not for her, I should think. She had always thought of herself as a highflier."

"Then suddenly she takes up with the church. I find that very hard to explain—in someone who had specialized in the daring, the unorthodox, the *bold*."

George Wilson was enjoying a creamy and custardy dessert, and he went on eating to get his thoughts in order.

"I don't know her well enough to comment, but I can

think of a couple of points you ought to take into consideration. First of all, it's still only recently that women have been admitted to the clergy. It's new, trailblazing, even theatrical. So to that extent it *was* a bold move."

"Yes, I made that point to Evelyn Southwell."

"*She'd* know all about theatrical . . . God rest her soul. Second, my old dad used to say that the church was one career where you could get ahead without an ounce of brainpower or common sense or judgment. I seem to remember he used to add: 'same applies to the police and the army,' but a lot has happened in those bodies since his time. Anyway, maybe women in the church are enjoying their power and influence, their place in the community, and some of them—maybe like Jean Mannering—who never found their place in industry, administration or whatever have taken flight to the church and maybe found their niche there. I don't suppose Jean would see it like that herself, though."

"What kind of career has she had in the C of E?"

"I only know what I read in the papers. Seems to have done pretty well for herself. She had a parish for a bit—somewhere in the Dewsbury area, I think—and then she got a special job of being flown in, so to speak, to parishes with unexpected vacancies, problems and so on. This was quite a high-profile job, and it was a way of using her to best advantage before she reached retirement age, which she won't do for another three or four years. Bishoprics are out for women, as I'm sure you know, but there's been talk of her going on synod or convocation or the House of Holy Toffs or whatever the top body is called."

"And there hasn't been a problem with her being lesbian?"

"Not so far as I know, which is what I read in the paper. Silent as the grave. Perhaps she's assured them that it's in the past. That's what several homosexuals have said, isn't it? 'Yes, we used to, but now we've attained a state of chastity.' Ee—these religious people tie themselves up in knots sometimes, don't they?"

"About sex they do," said Eve, not feeling qualified to go any further. "I wonder why sex looms so much larger in their thinking than the other sins. But we haven't talked about her emotional life."

"That's because I know nowt—except of course what I heard as gossip, and like I said, that wasn't much. People lost interest. But there was talk about a succession of 'partners,' both before and after London, and during too I would guess, wouldn't you? When she started studying for the church, I imagine she got more circumspect. I haven't heard the slightest bit of gossip, that's what makes me think that. The reason I know there was always a 'best friend' goes back to the days when her mother and father ran the corner shop in Drake Street. With close friends they used to gossip a bit, and when they did, of course it got around. Just before they moved down south—"

"When would that be?"

"Oh, early eighties maybe. Just before that they said to somebody that Jean always had a current best friend, and either she broke them in, and then lost interest in them, or they rebelled and moved out. She may have changed when she 'got God,' but I wouldn't put my money on it, would you?"

No, Eve thought. Though she had to admit that, judging by the present-day Jean Mannering, she didn't see the magnetism and vital attraction of the woman. Perhaps religion *had* turned her conventional.

Detective Constable Omkar Rani was halfway through the second of the corridored sections of Autumn Prospect when he came upon Mrs. Lancaster, who was delighted her turn was come.

"I've been watching you," she said. "Through a crack in my door. You've been *ages*. You didn't see me, did you?"

"No, I didn't," said Rani. "You must have been clever about it."

"Oh I am. You have to be here. The slightest thing and some of them complain. I'm Dora Lancaster, by the way. Dorothea on the birth certificate. Everyone here calls me 'Old Mrs. Lancaster,' which is nonsense when 'old' is what all of us are."

"Of course it is. How did it come about?"

"My son married a flashy woman who makes a bit of a stir in Bradford social circles. Talk about a big fish in diminishing waters! So I became 'old' Mrs. Lancaster long before I came here . . . You're a good-looking boy."

"Thank you. And you're a good-looking lady."

"Good looking doesn't apply after seventy-five. We've got our minds on other things, and so have our nearest and dearest: who's going to get the loot?" She cackled. "It won't be young Mrs. Lancaster or her foolish husband, I can tell you that. So what do you want?"

"I want to talk about the day Mrs. Southwell died."

"Well, I guessed that. I told the other policeman who

came around what I was doing that day. He was very off-hand, and seemed to have made up his mind that none of us could have done it. Probably thought we were too feeble to have held the pillow down. So I just answered the questions he asked and nothing else."

Rani looked at her, and she looked back almost flirtatiously.

"I'd better see if I can ask some other questions, then, hadn't I?"

"You could try asking questions about Evelyn."

"All right: how did you get on with Mrs. Southwell?"

"Not badly. Quite well really. We'd both got all our marbles, which is more than can be said for some of them here. Of course she was a show-off, and basically a rather silly person, because everything had to come back to herself. But you could have a conversation with her, and that's a bit of a miracle because topics of conversation don't abound in places like this."

"I suppose they don't. When was the last time you had a real conversation with Mrs. Southwell?"

"On the afternoon of the day she was murdered. Say four thirty to five."

Rani's eyebrows rose, and so did his heart.

"That's very exact."

"I always have my tea at four thirty. Everyone knows that and knows that's the time to call on me. Evelyn did that quite often: she liked tea and a biscuit, or a piece of cake or a little sandwich. It makes a break in the day."

"So she came in and had a cup of tea, something to eat, and you talked?"

"Yes."

"Had she come because there was something she wanted to talk about?"

"Yes. Or that was my impression. She'd had a visit from a woman. Or not exactly a visit. Not a social call."

"What sort of a call then?"

"You might say a snooping one." She cackled again. "More like a visit from the social services. A lot of do-gooders they are, who do precious little good when it comes down to it."

"Did the visitor say she was from the DSS?"

"Not really. She came about lunchtime or just after and flashed some kind of ID with her photograph on it. She said there were worries about security."

"Oh really. What kind of worries? Did she say?"

"Worries about keys getting into the wrong hands."

"So what did she propose to do about that?"

"She wanted to take a record of Evelyn's keys, so that if an identical one turned up, it could be identified."

Rani pondered this gnomic rationale.

"Well, I can see why Mrs. Southwell might have been worried," he said.

"She gave over the keys readily enough, but then she started thinking. Wouldn't it have been better to change the locks? The woman came back in twenty minutes, said they had a record of both of them now and she needn't worry, because she was perfectly safe."

"Was that all?"

"Yes. She marched out when Evelyn started to ask her questions."

"And did Mrs. Southwell say what she looked like? Did she know her?"

"Oh no. She didn't know her, not even by sight. She said she was a typical social worker—fairly efficient and usually sympathetic but no time to be anything more than that. The sort who can't wait to be gone, but usually disguise it pretty well. We all know the type here."

Rani liked Mrs. Lancaster and thought that, for all her age and infirmities, she would make a superb witness in the box. He thanked her, and went on his way full of hope that he was on to something. He first went around to the other two detective constables doing their run-of-the-mill job from door to door. None of them had been told about a social worker who was worried about keys and security. They both agreed to ask specifically from then on, and to check with the residents they had already talked to. Then Rani strolled over to the porter's lodge.

"Did you happen to have any social workers visiting patients on the day Mrs. Southwell died?" he asked. The porter flicked back the pages of his visitors' book and peered at the entry.

"We call them residents, not patients, young fellow. Mrs. Ellenborough called to see Mr. Baxter. He won't be with us long. Miss Tonstall visited Mrs. Walton."

"When was this?"

"First at half past ten. Left at a quarter to eleven. The second at ten past eleven, left at a quarter past."

"Anyone come at lunchtime or just after?"

"No, just the two that whole day. That's pretty much par for the course."

"Any other visitors—family, friends—around lunchtime?"

"No. That's not a usual time to visit. There was one at a quarter to twelve, then not another till ten to four."

"Were you here in your lodge all the time during lunch hour?"

He peered down again.

"No. I note when something comes up. Security isn't top-notch here because there's only me, or my relief at nights. We do try to put up a show of efficiency, though. I was out for ten minutes to see Mr. Baxter, who'd been upset by the social worker. That was one thirty to forty. Then out again when I went to replenish the stock of blankets. That was from two fifteen to two forty. Then I was on duty continuous till I finished at five."

"Did you see anyone around? Anyone who might be apparently loitering but really was keeping an eye on you to see if you left your post?"

He thought. Rani guessed he was slow but thorough.

"There was a woman. Neat and tidy. Went to the hair-dresser's regularly, or did her own very cleverly. My missus was a hairdresser, so I notice. Light makeup or none at all I'd guess, though I was too far away to be sure."

"Clothes?"

"Short jacket, sensible design, probably waterproof, beige color, then an old-fashioned sort of skirt, just below the knees, and flat shoes. Didn't look the sort to loiter, but she was sort of shilly-shallying around."

"What do you mean? What did she do?"

"Well, she passed the entrance slowly, and I took notice, but not particular notice, but then she came back past the door, walking a little faster, and I wondered what she could have been doing, because there's no shops along there, only houses, and she didn't seem to have had the time to have made a proper call. The last I saw of her she was on the other side of the road, going through the gate of that house over there—that one, see?—with the for sale notice up. Then I went to do the blankets."

Bingo! thought Rani.

CHAPTER 13

The Impostor

"So let's sum up: what do we have so far?" Superintendent Collins asked Rani, when he had listened to his account of his talk with Mrs. Lancaster. "First and most important the fact that Evelyn Southwell had a visit, during the afternoon of the day she died, from someone probably posing as an emissary of the DSS or some other branch of the social services. In the course of the visit, the woman took Mrs. Southwell's keys, returning them later."

"That's the important point, isn't it?" Rani put in.

"Oh yes. Since the porter seems to have known little about her beyond her appearance, and since she seems to have done the same to none of the other residents, that was obviously the purpose of her visiting Mrs. Southwell. I must admit I did have a twinge of doubt while you were telling me."

"Why was that, sir?"

"It seemed such a rotten story. Couldn't she have come up with anything better? But then I thought that any story, however convincing, had the same drawback: if the woman was legitimate why hadn't she got the relevant keys from the porter? That way she would have avoided disturbing a vulnerable old person—Southwell may not have seemed particularly vulnerable, but old people always have a greater stock of worries than the rest of us because they are comparatively weak, mentally and physically."

"And the answer to your question, sir, is that the porter would be much more reluctant to give up keys, even temporarily, without making a thorough check on the person asking and the reason for the request. Not to mention that the porter would have been able to give a physical description of the visitor to us after the murder."

"Exactly. Mrs. Southwell only began to have doubts after she had given up the keys, and she quite soon got them back. The whole incident became something to talk about at tea time. *Anything* happening in an old people's home becomes a topic of conversation."

"Yes, sir. And in fact Mrs. Southwell doesn't seem to have had any serious doubt that the visitor was a member of the social services. I suppose we've got to remember that we're probably dealing with an actress. And with someone who, in her job as traveling vicar, no doubt deals a lot with the social services and has had many opportunities to observe their manner and their ways of approaching old people."

Collins shot him a glance, and remained sunk in thought.

"Are we, though?" he said at length. "Dealing, I mean, with someone who is both a vicar and actress—both sides of a saucy joke. I need convincing that we are. Do we have any reason to associate Evelyn Southwell's murder with someone whose path crossed with hers, if it ever did, thirty-odd years before?"

Rani nodded, but confidently. He had had longer to think of this than Collins.

"I'd say there is a reason for thinking a connection is likely, sir. Mrs. Southwell had had a visit from Eve McNabb a few days before. They had discussed those happenings you mention of thirty-odd years before. That same evening Eve rang Jean Mannering and told her the gist of the conversation. How many visitors do you think Southwell had in a month? Maybe several when she had that eighty-fifth birthday, but I bet that's all died down." He thought, then added shamefacedly: "I should have asked the porter."

"No harm done." Collins jumped up and went to the door. He barked to the newest recruit to the detective force: "Ring Autumn Prospect, an old people's setup in Keighley. Talk to the porter. Ask how many visitors—recorded visitors—Evelyn Southwell had had in the four weeks before her death."

He came back into his office and sat down.

"Okay. This is definitely something that needs to be looked into. But we mustn't forget that there might be a hundred and one things in Evelyn Southwell's private or professional life that are much more important, much more likely to lead to murder."

"Yes, sir. But we ought also to ask, if such a thing turns up, why it has suddenly become important when Southwell was in her last years."

"Fair enough . . ." Collins thought, then said: "The reason I'm uneasy is that this business of getting John

McNabb out of May's life is not only way in the past. It's also the fact that it never became a criminal matter, or even a matter of any kind of importance. It was successful. John tamely packed his bags and went. If the police had been called in, they might have arrested Jean later on a charge of wasting police time or some kind of minor conspiracy, but it wouldn't have been worse than that. Why has the incident become important now?"

The serious-minded face of the new detective constable poked itself around the door.

"No recorded visits to Mrs. Southwell, other than Miss McNabb's, in the month before she died, sir."

"Thank you, Ackley."

Collins chewed at imaginary gum in his mouth.

"Now let's get her method straight in our minds. She—the woman observed by the porter—studies Autumn Prospect at lunchtime and takes advantage of the porter's absences. Probably she doesn't know she's been spotted. Then she comes back at night. By then your man had clocked off, hadn't he?"

"Oh yes. But the night porter has been talked to, as soon as doubts were raised about the death. He usually watches television and dozes most evenings if nothing comes up. The night nurse, if she spots anything unusual, goes around to see that everything's all right. It's usually just lights left on. That's what happened in this case, around about ten o'clock, when she found Southwell alive and asleep. The porter went around at eleven, checked all the outside doors, then locked the main door and went to sleep in his chair, dozing off and waking at odd times through the night."

"If only he'd locked the main door first, then gone and checked up around the flats."

"True. Our man suggested that. The porter protested that he might have had to unlock the door and let a late visitor out."

"Tough. Anyway, it doesn't seem as though Autumn Prospect is plagued by many visitors at any time of the day, let alone late at night."

"Well, that's when the murderer will have got out, sir: late at night when the porter was doing his rounds."

"All this suggests that some reconnaissance was done in the days leading up to the murder. She—or he—established there was a routine, and took advantage of it."

"That may account for the gap between Eve McNabb ringing up Jean Mannering and the actual committing of the murder."

Collins sighed.

"You won't give up on our lady vicar, will you, Rani? Are lady vicars particularly prone to homicide?"

"Not so far as I know, sir. But reputation, a stainless career to put on the resumé, must be very important to the clergy."

Collins had heard talk in the police canteen about Rani and Eve, and now risked a reference to it.

"What is your lady friend doing at the moment, Rani?"

"She was going to talk to a retired teacher from Blackfield Road this morning. We're supposed to be meeting when I finish my shift in ten minutes."

"Well, why don't you bring her up here for a chat before you go gallivanting or whatever you plan on doing? Just in case something has come up."

Robert Barnard

Rani nodded, and as soon as he had gone, Collins glanced at his case notes and phoned a number in the Huddersfield area. When he got a recorded message giving a mobile number, he rang that.

"Yes?" A warm, concerned voice, not at all offhand or bossy.

"Is that the Reverend Mannering?"

"It is."

"Ah. This is Chief Superintendent Collins of the Leeds CID."

"What can I help you with, Chief Superintendent?"

"I wanted to have a word with you about the death of Mrs. Evelyn Southwell." There was a silence. "I believe you knew the lady years ago when you both lived in Crossley."

"I knew *of* her, Superintendent. I don't recall that our paths ever crossed. I'd actually been to the Blackfield Road Primary as a tot, but that was before her time."

"Yes, and before Mrs. McNabb's time too. You did know Mrs. McNabb quite well, didn't you?"

"Oh yes. She was a lovely person. It was terrible to hear of her death recently. Sixty-seven is no great age these days, is it?"

"No, it's not. I believe her daughter, Eve, rang you recently after she'd talked to Mrs. Southwell."

"That's right, she did." Again a silence. Collins registered that the voice was beginning to sound less warm.

"I wonder if I could come and talk to you. Or if you could come yourself to Leeds and talk to me here."

"I'm in Bradford at the moment . . . I think the best thing would be for me to come over. Is it Millgarth?

Right. I'll ask at the desk for you. If I can find parking, it won't take long."

Collins thanked her and put the phone down. He deputed Ackley to meet her at the desk and take her to one of the more cheerful interview rooms. Then he greeted Rani and Eve.

"Thanks for coming. I remember saying we should keep in touch so that I knew anything you knew. Come into my office so you can tell me about your talk with this teacher."

"There's not much to tell of a factual nature," said Eve, settling into an armchair, with Rani behind her. "But we did talk about some things that fill in the background of the characters concerned. George Wilson is a retired teacher, and he's lived in Crossley most of his life. Inevitably he knew Jean Mannering, and he worked for Mrs. Southwell and I learned a lot about her."

"And the community?" pressed Collins. "I'd be interested in hearing whether people in the village knew about Mannering's lesbianism, and how they reacted."

"Yes, we did talk about that. A split reaction, as you might expect. For example, when Jean's parents told her it was time she moved away from home, most of the village assumed it was her sexual orientation they were objecting to, and some thought they were being very old-fashioned in reacting like that. George, though, thought the parents were fed up with being bossed around and organized in their own home."

"She's a control freak, then?"

"Yes, or was then. And this got into her other personal relationships. There were a string of these, and George said either Jean gained the control that she yearned for and then over time lost interest—"

"Why? No challenge any longer?"

"Something like that, I should think. Or else she was unsuccessful, the partner didn't want a role as an underling, and she moved on."

"I see." Collins thought for a moment. "Did Mr. Wilson know much about Jean's career in the church?"

"No, not a great deal, though he sometimes read about her in the paper. Crossley takes the *Halifax Guardian*. I expect if he'd seen the Huddersfield paper regularly he'd have seen the name a lot more often. She's currently a sort of roving stand-in around the Yorkshire parishes, and is tipped for a seat or place in general synod or convocation or some such body. Sorry to be vague, but I was brought up to be vague about religion. And I don't think the C of E means any more to George than it does to me. He just has a general sense that she's done pretty well and is highly thought of."

"Well," said Collins, getting up, "a good name is always worth hanging on to, and a lot of good names conceal a shadow life of one kind or another. Look at politicians. Sometimes churches are like politicians: they have a great deal of covering up to do—or feel that they have to. In some cases I feel the high-ups ought to be charged with conspiracy. I'm thinking about concealing abuse against children by clergymen. But that's beside the point. It still seems as if we're a long way from a motive for murder."

Eve and Rani got up.

"I've got her coming to talk to me, by the way," Collins said, leading the way out. "Ackley's fetching her up."

"Who? Jean Mannering?" asked Eve.

"The same. I got her on her mobile and she's coming over from Bradford."

They came out of a corridor, on to a wide, airy landing with a view down to the ground floor just below. As they all idled along, talking about Evelyn Southwell, a door opened below them and coming through and aiming for the interview rooms, Eve saw a young detective, obviously newish and eager to please or make some impression of a positive kind. With him was a woman in a gray skirt and a god collar over shirt and dark stockings. She was talking politely and relaxedly but in low tones, and Eve caught only a few words.

"I do get many more people saying how much they welcome women to positions of influence in the church than I hear from people who curse the day it happened. But then I suppose I would . . ."

The last word faded as they walked toward swing doors and out of hearing. Eve swung around and looked at Superintendent Collins. He nodded his head.

"That's her," he said.

"But it's not," said Eve. "That woman is definitely not Jean Mannering."

CHAPTER 14

The Worshipper

The woman who now disappeared from their sight had been confident, unfazed by her surroundings and very attractive. She had made an entrance like an actress, and she had conducted polite and intelligent conversation with the rookie policeman with admirable interest and concern for him. She was everything that an actress turned vicar should be.

Eve turned to Superintendent Collins. He looked irritated, but also keen to get to the bottom of things.

"I must go and talk to her," he muttered. Rani and Eve looked at each other, turned, went downstairs, then out to Rani's car in silence—companionable, thoughtful silence.

They had been driving four or five miles on the road to Crossley when Eve broke the silence. She said to Rani:

"Would you be willing to drive me to Huddersfield?"

"Yes," said Rani without a moment's hesitation, changing course at the next convenient turnoff and driving with his usual confident insouciance. "I won't ask what you're intending to do."

"No, don't. And don't stay with me, or too near me. I don't want to be responsible for getting you officially rebuked, or to hold back your career in any way. What a beginning that would be for us! Just keep well away."

"We'll think about that when we arrive. You haven't told me yet where we are going."

"It's a suburb called Heckford, a couple of miles from the center. The house is 23 Portland Gardens. Leave me around a corner maybe, or a fair way away."

"I know the street," said Rani. "We had a gang bust-up near there that looked like a domestic but blew up into something big. I'll keep well away from the house."

"I wonder what they are doing," agonized Eve. "What she is telling them . . . I like your Superintendent Collins. I think he will understand what is happening."

As they neared Huddersfield, Eve said: "I keep seeing the doorbells. Naylor, Dougall and Mannering. Top to bottom. I wonder if she'll be in . . ."

When they got to Portland Gardens, Rani peered at the numbers, and when they had decreased to the fifties he turned up into a side street and parked the car.

"You could go down the parallel street at the back," he said, pointing. "See—there where that man is turning off. You might be seen from the kitchen window, but it's better than being seen from a great distance. Go down two blocks and then take the road back to Portland Gardens. And *be careful.*"

In spite of her declared determination not to involve Rani, Eve was comforted by his evident understanding of what she was about to do, and how she had worked out the situation.

"Of course I will," she said, getting out of the car. "I don't think she will pose a threat."

"But remember she's a—" But the car door shut and she was gone. Rani shook his head, but felt that he did not need to remind Eve of what she was.

She turned off out of his view and walked down the street parallel to Portland Gardens. After two blocks she turned into another connecting road and made her way back to the Gardens that had no gardens. She threw a quick look around her, remembered number 23, then walked up to it, through the gate and up toward the three doorbells. She stood before them for a moment, then rang the lowest one. She listened, and was sure the ringing was in the ground-floor flat. Then she heard footsteps coming downstairs, and the front door opened.

"Oh, Miss McNabb."

There was not a great deal of surprise in the tone.

"Yes. Can I come in?"

"Well, I don't . . . Yes, yes of course. Mind the stairs. The carpet is getting rather frayed."

She led the way up, and Eve could not see her face. When she opened the door to the flat and let her in she did not gesture to the chairs as she had before, but just stood with her back against the door, her face questioning.

"You wanted to speak to me?"

Eve looked around her, slowly.

"Yes . . . I wondered which flat you would take me to. I suppose you can hear the bell ringing downstairs from here."

"I don't see what—"

"I think you probably know that Jean Mannering is currently at the police headquarters in Leeds, being questioned about the murder of Evelyn Southwell. That does alter the situation, doesn't it, Miss Dougall?"

The face began to crumble. Then she walked unsteadily across the room and sank into an armchair. The first words she spoke seemed to Eve quite irrelevant, except that she was putting off talking.

"I couldn't take you downstairs, not the first time, or now. It's full of photographs of Jean in her parts with the drama groups she's acted with. Wonderful photographs: Judith Bliss in *Hay Fever*; Nora in *A Doll's House*; Mrs. Danvers; Miss Jean Brodie. Also one with the archbishop of Canterbury. You would have realized that was Jean, and I wasn't her."

"Yes, I would."

"It all began with such an innocent mistake . . . Well, not even a mistake really, except that Jean is so . . ." She turned and looked at Eve, a penetrating look, as if willing her to believe. "We've been together—or not exactly together, but spiritually so—for a long time now, but we're still in love. I love her quite as much as when we first realized we had something special between us. Long ago. It was soon after Jean came back up north. She was leading the chorus of women in *Murder in the Cathedral*. I was one of them. I've always been a Christian. It has made sense of my life, made me understand why God made me so different. His purpose through me. Jean was so different from me, but yet the same. We seemed just made for each other. And we *were*."

The last was said fiercely. Eve, mindful of her duties as a possible police employee, said: "I think you should be saying this at the station." Miss Dougall looked at her, disconcerted, fearful.

"Do we have to? *Now?*"

Eve looked at her in the most schoolmistressy manner she knew of, inherited from her mother.

"You realize that Jean is being interrogated as a suspect for Mrs. Southwell's murder. It will be very frightening for her."

"Yes . . . Though nothing frightens Jean . . . Can I put a coat on?"

While she fetched a coat from the hall, Eve rang the duty sergeant at Millgarth.

"Will you tell Superintendent Collins that I'm coming in with Miss Dougall, Jean Mannering's partner. And will you ring DC Rani on his mobile and tell him to fetch me. He knows where."

Miss Dougall came back in, looking quite composed now in a coat of pinky beige, and they went slowly down the stairs.

"I suppose I won't see the old place for a long time," she said. "We've been so happy here. Together but not together. The church would not have been at all pleased. It was all like a game, a lovely children's game!"

She moved down the narrow stairs with the confidence of long use of them. As she continued forward through the front door, Eve thought there was something queenly about her, and then changed her mind: it was something actressy. Perhaps the stage techniques of her lover had somewhat rubbed off on her. Then she remembered that the church often attracted people by its ceremonial, its costumes, its pageantry.

Rani drove up as they went through the gate, and Eve put Miss Dougall in the back and then herself slipped in the other side. As Rani drove off she took up the conversation from where they had left it.

"You haven't told me how Miss Mannering became interested in religion. Was it acting in the play that led her to the church?"

"Oh yes, partly," said Dougie brightly. "And partly me. And partly the fact that women were taking a tremendous step forward in the church at that time. It was so splendid to talk about it, wonder whether Jean could be a part of it!"

"Those must have been exciting times for you. So Jean wanted to be part of that movement, did she?"

"Oh yes, she did! She was just finishing an Open University course at the time, and she got time off work to study the theological and historical part of the requirements for ordination. She said it was just to have 'another string to my bow,' but I always hoped it would be more than that, and thank God it caught her imagination. It was awfully exciting, for me as well as for her."

"You never thought of entering the priesthood yourself?"

She shook her head vigorously.

"Oh no. I don't have the brains. My mother always told me I wasn't likely to go far in anything that needed brains, and she was right. I could deal with people's practical problems—I was a social worker, so I'd spent my whole life doing that—but spiritual ones I couldn't begin to advise them about. Jean could, and I found it wonderful playing a small part in what happened. Of course it meant changes in our lives . . ."

"Had you been living together?"

"Oh yes. And we changed that. Jean said she saw nothing wrong in it, but it would be a terrible distraction if the newspapers got on to it. The church could probably tolerate the situation, she said, if they swallowed hard, but it would divert attention from important things and make her work much more difficult. So thereafter we lived close to each other but not *with* each other. I didn't find it sad. It was more exciting—as I said, like a game."

"The present situation seems ideal," said Eve.

"Yes, it is," said Dougie, turning to her with a quite charming smile. "The top flat is usually let to a student. They have very little interest in anyone but themselves. They always know that we're close, and any message for Jean can be given to me. I retired from social work two years ago."

"And Jean's 'calling'—is that the word?—has been a great success, people say."

"Oh, it has. First in her parish, then in the new troubleshooter role. She's much loved, I can tell you that. So often she's asked, when she's sorted out a parish and got things on to an even keel, if she couldn't take it on, but she's always said the change from parish to parish suits her, and she wouldn't give it up for the world. There's a very good chance of her being elected to general synod."

Miss Dougall said this last very proudly, as if it were an assured place in the heavenly choir. Eve thought she detected signs of mania in the voice, and in the eyes, but thought she had probably known too few really religious people.

"And all this time the business of getting rid of my father has been hanging over her."

Dougie shot Eve a glance.

"You know about it? It's been hanging over both of us."

"When did you learn of it?"

"Oh, while she was studying for the priesthood. She said she wanted to make a clean breast of it. But in fact she told me very little then. How did you learn about it?"

"I talked about it with my father in Australia."

"Your father? So at least he's—"

"Not dead? No, he's not dead."

"Jean heard the general talk, and assumed he was dead. She has always been afraid he committed suicide. Small things can have such terrifyingly large consequences. It was a silly thing to do, and quite out of character for Jean. She went and removed the . . . the stuff herself from your house."

"After my father had flown to Australia."

"Yes, but . . . Oh, she was so ashamed of herself! She only told me the full details recently."

"I think she should be ashamed. Tell me how it came about. How she says it came about."

She was looked at as if she had suggested something dirty.

"Oh, Jean never tells me a lie. If she says it, it's true. She was desperate to get rid of John from May's life. She says he was an irrelevance. May could never settle down into a single-sex relationship because John was always around. He had become a fixture in her life, Jean felt, without May any longer feeling any love for him. But he was the father of her child—you—and unless he was somehow got rid of, May would never get the full pleasure of their love for each other."

"If May felt that love in the same way."

"Oh, Jean was quite sure she did, and *could* in an even greater way."

"And the weekend when they were both away, May and John, presented Jean with a wonderful opportunity."

"Exactly. She felt she had to use it. She had the run of your house from the Friday morning, when your mother left for her conference in Birmingham. Jean was to feed the cat."

"McGonagall. I remember him from much later. He lived to be a highly respected elder-statesman cat."

"So she got together a collection of . . . stuff . . . I find this highly distasteful—"

"How did she get it together?"

"Oh, there was no problem about that, I can assure you. Pictures of young girls appeal to both sexes, in fact. *Elements* in both sexes, I should say. It's something I intensely dislike. Jean does too."

Ho ho, Eve thought.

"Anyway she stowed the porno magazines in a wardrobe in the spare bedroom and that was all that needed doing, apart from ringing your father in his hotel and getting him on the plane, with the ticket she had booked, which was being held for him at Heathrow."

"Wasn't she just a bit apprehensive that he'd laugh at the whole business?"

"Oh she was. It was touch and go."

"What would she have done if he had?"

"Jean assured me she would never have rung the police in earnest. She would just have gone and removed the pornography."

Hardly worth putting it there in the first place, Eve thought. This from Jean Mannering, who never told her partner a lie. She left a brief silence.

"But in fact my father caved in to the whole blackmailing scheme."

"Yes. You use unkind words, but Jean was convinced he almost welcomed her ultimatum. She thinks that it solved a problem he had been wrestling with but was undecided about. The situation with Jean and your mother cannot have been good for his vanity."

"Leave his vanity out of it. My father has as little vanity as any man I know." Eve's tone had become tart. "The situation was quite simply bad for everyone. And Jean was quite wrong about my mother's feeling for her as things turned out, wasn't she?"

"Yes," said Miss Dougall reluctantly.

"Tell me about the phone call."

"Well, Jean had been talking that evening at the Sapphonics club. They had an early evening lecture, then dancing, fun and games, or whatever. After the talk, which was on women in business, she went and phoned your father twice before she got through. The Sapphonics had a little office in the Co-op Social Club building where the meetings were held, and she used that, since she was on the committee. First your father couldn't believe his ears, then he swore at her, then he said the police wouldn't be interested, which wasn't true."

"No. The police are still very interested in Internet child pornography," said Rani from the front seat. "And even more so if that's possible when the child model is obviously being abused in some way, which is often the case."

"*Don't!*" said Miss Dougall, shuddering. "Anyway, after a time your father believed her, was convinced she was serious, and in the end said he'd be on the plane. Jean said he'd better be because that was something that would be monitored, and the child pornography would only be removed after he had flown out."

"And that was that?"

Dougie looked down into her lap, and spoke low.

"Not quite. When she had finished the phone call, she left the office and found Evelyn Southwell standing outside, grinning. 'Well done,' she said; 'you've solved a knotty problem. We'll both be the better for it, and May will be too. Like me to go down to Heathrow and do the monitoring? It's the sort of thing I'd enjoy.' Anyway, they talked, sparred a bit, but in the end Jean was dead tired, emotionally and physically, and she told Evelyn all the details and let her go to Heathrow. In the morning about ten she heard from her that he'd gone through passport control and presumably got on the plane."

"But that wasn't the end of it?" asked Eve.

"Well no, it wasn't. How did you know?"

"It never is."

"I suppose the torment went on because getting involved gave Evelyn a power over Jean, who had thought the plan up and done the really culpable things. It wasn't much, but if they ever met, Evelyn would make some allusion to what had happened, to their both being in it together, to the ruse having been brilliantly effective. Then, later, it was how Evelyn's conscience was troubling her, and how interested the church would be if they got to hear about Jean. It was so sad: the woman Jean would love to have heard from would have nothing to do with her—she would not even reply to the letters Jean sent once a year on the anniversary of their meeting. And the woman she could only associate with an episode she was bitterly ashamed of she met now and again and always got sly threats and reminders of the past. But of course for some time they hadn't met: Evelyn Southwell had been in Autumn Prospect for over two years, and the articles when she was eighty-five hadn't thrown up any lightly disguised threats."

"Was Jean Mannering expecting them to?"

"I don't suppose she knew Mrs. Southwell was approaching eighty-five, or that there would be local interest. I know when she saw the piece in the *Halifax Guardian* she read it carefully and was very relieved when there was nothing in it that could remotely refer to her."

"She read a lot of the local papers, did she?" asked Eve.

"Yes, as background to her work. But she never read any one regularly because she knew all areas of Yorkshire and had worked in many of them as a troubleshooter. So she just picked up one or another paper when she saw them in the shop."

"That's presumably why she didn't know about my mother's death when so many other friends and acquaintances had already written with condolences."

"Yes, that was the reason. She just hadn't seen copies of the *Halifax Guardian* that had the death notice and the piece about your mother. If she had, and if I hadn't run out of milk one morning, all this would not have happened."

She looked beseechingly at Eve, and Eve read in her face a sort of pleading, as if she was saying: "Can't we forget all this, so that I can go back to the lovely and cozy life I've been living with Jean?" It was a pleading that knew it could not realistically nourish hope. But it gave Eve a vivid picture of Dougie as one of those religious people who loved submitting themselves to things—the church—or to people—Jean.

"Milk?" said Eve in a businesslike voice.

"Yes. It *was* all my fault, and all my doing. You must realize that Jean had nothing to do with any of it. I usually go down to the shops just before my lunchtime, if I'm at home. Well, you'd know that, wouldn't you, my dear? That's when you first saw me, didn't you? And I posted that second letter to you on the way."

"Yes, I saw that."

"Well, on the day of the first letter, I found we'd run out of milk at breakfast time, and I do like my cornflakes or Frosties, so I went down to the supermarket and on the way I posted that letter of Jean's to your mother. I do almost all of Jean's professional correspondence these days, and as a rule I'd post it when I went to the shop around twelve. I didn't think twice about posting this one earlier. I knew who it was to. Jean did all her personal letters herself, and sometimes I felt just a teeny-weeny bit jealous that once a year she would write a little note to your mother, to keep in touch. I always knew, and had come to accept, that May was the great love of Jean's life.

She'd written to her regularly, and never put her own address on because it wasn't necessary: May knew it. The letters were their only contact."

"So what happened?"

"About eleven Jean rang and said: 'You haven't been to the post yet, I suppose?' I was caught on the hop and I said 'no,' and Jean said she was in Crossley, talking to the vicar about an appeal to restore a fine stained-glass window in the church, and she'd heard about May's death from him. She told me to hold the letter back and destroy it."

"That must have put you on the spot."

"It did. I went down to the postbox, hoping to get it from the postman who collected it, but the collections aren't at regular times anymore, and the newsagent said it had already been done that morning, about ten thirty, so there was nothing I could do. I confessed to Jean that evening, in fear and trembling, said I was muddled and had forgotten the trip to the shop at breakfast time, and that it had already gone. Jean was very stern. She must have realized I had lied to her, and of course I realized there must have been something of a sexual nature, something compromising, in the letter."

"Jean could have rung me and asked me not to read the letter," said Eve. "I would have been intrigued, but I wouldn't have peeped."

"We thought of that, but then Jean realized there had been no address on the letter or envelope, and no surname. We thought anyway you could have decided not to open any letters addressed to your mother—too intrusive when she had just died. Eventually Jean decided there could be no harm in a formal letter of con-dolence to you, which she would naturally have sent if the other letter had not been written, and very much wanted to do."

"But I suppose you weren't happy with the situation."

"No. I didn't want the second letter to be written, and I didn't think there was necessarily not going to be fallout from the first. But I accepted it was Jean's decision, and of course she saw it should not be associated with the first letter, so I wrote it, as I usually do. We went over it to see that the tone was right, and the next day I posted it as you saw . . . I don't know what you know about social work."

"Not much. Why do you ask?"

"I was a social worker, and more often than you would think, we get threats, minor violence, being stalked. You get alert to the possibility that you are being followed. I realized the day you came over to Huddersfield that you were on my tail. By the time I got to the shops, I'd noticed you. I even got a good look at you from inside the super-market. I was on the alert from then on. I already knew you were back when I heard the bell ringing in the down-stairs flat. I had decided what I would do. I would *be* Jean, prove the handwriting on the first letter was not mine, and the whole nasty business would be forgotten."

She spoke of this extraordinary decision precisely, like a royal personage delivering an anodyne speech written for her by someone else. Indeed she could almost be talking of someone else, except for those piercing eyes.

"Brave of you, in a way," said Eve.

"Brave?"

Robert Barnard

"This wouldn't please Jean Mannering."

"It didn't when she found out. She's such a *straight* person, so totally honest." And a right tartar to people she's got under her thumb, thought Eve. "But when it seemed that my little trick had worked, then she calmed down about it. We didn't hear any more from you for a while, and we thought you must have accepted that this dreadful Aunt Ada had been responsible. She'd always had a bee in her bonnet about Jean and your mother."

"She does seem like a survival from another age."

"But then of course you rang after you'd talked to Mrs. Southwell. You got through to the number I gave you, and Jean, who was in my flat, answered the phone. I suppose that must have been the only occasion you've talked to her."

"I suppose so. Not the last though."

"You'll love her if you can talk the situation over. Everyone loves her. Anyway, she got me—the 'Jean Mannering' you were used to—and I coped as best as I could."

"You coped very well. I had no suspicions."

"But then you struck chill into my heart with your talk about Evelyn Southwell making further trouble in the future, and enjoying all the publicity she would get. I knew you were judging the situation absolutely rightly. Jean had told me that was how she had always been. I was used to the type. You see, for most of my years as a social worker, I concentrated on old people."

"Really?"

"So I *know* them—know all kinds, know the fears and hopes they all have in common. From what I'd heard about Mrs. Southwell from Jean, I knew she would be the kind who hated and resented being shuffled out of the limelight and hidden away from view in a home, even if it was a very good type of home. She had nothing but other old people to perform to, other ghetto dwellers. And I knew she would have had her appetite for publicity whetted by the press attention on her eighty-fifth. I knew what would be coming, and how Mrs. Southwell would enjoy it, and how Jean's life and career would suffer for it."

"But would she have? Revealed it, I mean. After all, Mrs. Southwell herself was involved in it, if only in a minor way."

"You forget that old people have nothing to lose. There was probably no crime committed by dear Jean, and certainly none by Evelyn Southwell. She could wallow in publicity and in the destruction of Jean's career. I tell you, I *know* old people."

Eve, who thought in this case she was right, just nodded.

"And I'll tell you another thing I know about old people: unless they have kept most of their faculties, which is very rare, they *hate* being in the position they are in—helpless, often friendless, lonely, with only a flickering screen for company and comfort. Always they wish they had died five, ten years earlier, when they still had some kind of life, and above all still had their mental faculties and hadn't retreated into delusions. Often they know they have delusions, but can't rid themselves of them. The state, the law, are *vile* to old people. Dogs and cats are treated better."

"You mean they are put down?"

"Yes. Anyone who has worked with old people knows

that what they want most of all is to be allowed to die with dignity. And yet politicians always speak as if what old people want is to live longer. What utter fools they are!"

Eve left a moment's silence, and then asked: "Have you ever been tempted to intervene yourself?"

Miss Dougall threw her a look of cunning.

"I'd be a fool to tell you and your friend here if I had, wouldn't I? Let's just say I was often tempted."

"And here you had a personal rather than an altruistic reason to step in, didn't you?"

Dougie did not hesitate. She was into a full, obsessional confession.

"Yes, I did. Or at least personal *and* altruistic. I love the Anglican church—it's been my life, and I was responsible for making it Jean's as well. I feel so proud of everything she's done, and so excited about everything she's going to do. I had no choice but to do what I did. I was used to doing the donkey work of Jean's job, but I also did some of its more unpleasant duties as well, sometimes even did them without her knowing. All I wanted to do was help. Jean has a mannerism, quite unconscious, where she brushes away situations with her hand—like this—like brushing a book off a table. She did it more than once while we discussed your conversation with Mrs. Southwell. I knew she wanted me to cope—unconsciously she wanted that. So I just went ahead and did what needed to be done. The job chose me."

Oh no it didn't, thought Eve. You wanted it, and she wanted you to do it.

"But it was very dangerous, wasn't it?" she said. "You could so easily have been caught."

"Caught *then*? I suppose so. I didn't think of it. It came quite naturally to me. I wasn't *acting* a social worker, I was going back to *being* one, reverting to type. I talked to Mrs. Southwell just as I'd talked to hundreds, maybe thousands, of old people during my working lifetime. I'd watched Autumn Prospect, I knew the routines, and once I'd got the keys and taken the pattern of them, it was just a cinch. I went in, taking a torch, took up a spare pillow on her bed and pushed it down over her face. I'm quite strong—I've needed to be sometimes, working with helpless old women, often very large. It was so easy it must have been meant. I was out before the night porter had finished his rounds."

"And you didn't feel any compassion or guilt?"

"No. I felt good. I thought Mrs. Southwell would probably have thanked me."

"And what about when you got home?" asked Rani from the driving seat. "Didn't Jean Mannering want to know where you had been?"

"We don't live in each other's pockets. She'd had an evening meeting and went straight to bed when she came in. She didn't ask the next day what I'd been doing the night before, and I didn't tell her. We're two independent women."

"And you never discussed it later, when Mrs. Southwell's death got in the papers?"

"Oh, I think we just said 'poor woman,' or something like that."

Rani was negotiating the Leeds traffic system, and the two women behind him lapsed into silence. Eventually he slid the car into a small space outside Millgarth Police Headquarters and darted out to open doors. Eve was already out in the queasy afternoon sunlight, but Miss Dougall waited for Rani to open her door and then got out easily and smoothly, without the creaking bones and little moans of the old. She stood erect and self-possessed, waiting for them to give her directions, and Eve was struck by the change in her. She seemed to have immense dignity, a confident composure. She was not a criminal going for a crucial interview; she was a woman of good life who was satisfied that she had an achievement to her credit—something that many might criticize or misunderstand but which she could answer for, both to herself and to God. Was this madness, Eve wondered, or an advanced and perverse case of heroine worship? Or was it a part of the role she was playing—the impression she made on Eve was of an actress playing an actress—something she had learned to do from Jean Mannering?

They went up the steps and into the outer office of the station. People were sitting around singly or in little groups, waiting to make their complaints or meet their fates. Rani put his hand on Miss Dougall's arm and was about to steer her to the door that led to the offices, interview rooms and cells of the station proper when it opened. Through it came the woman whom Eve now knew was Jean Mannering, accompanied by the keen young detective constable. For a moment all five people froze in their places. Then Jean Mannering ran forward.

"Oh, Dougie! What have you done?"

LAST POST

The moment of Miss Dougall's greatness passed. She put her arms around her lover, her face on her shoulder, and sobbed into it. Suddenly she was diminished to a naughty schoolgirl who had done something beastly in the playground.

CHAPTER 15

The Truth

"So what's your take on Dougie's version?" Rani asked Eve.

They were at home in Derwent Road, and in the middle of a standard English meal of lamb chops and boiled potatoes. It was the first time that Rani had been properly home for any length of time since the scene in the reception area of Millgarth Police Headquarters. Eve had had plenty of time alone to mull over the situation, and she replied at once.

"I think Jean Mannering is unlikely to dispute her account," she said, with acid in her voice. "In fact she rubbed it in, or tried to, with her first words. 'What have you done?'—my foot! Thus cutting off any impulse Dougie may have later to implicate her as well."

Rani nodded.

"But I don't think Dougie will have any such impulse, do you?" he said. "She seemed utterly obsessed."

"Enchanted and enchained. But, by God, I'd love to find *some*thing that brought Jean into the picture."

"So would I. But I can't imagine her being so unwise as to commit anything to paper that we could use as evidence. She seemed streetwise to me."

"Oh, she would never do that in a million years. A mere gesture of irritation—that was all that was needed. But you're the one who has to think about trials, the Crown Prosecution Service and all that. If I get the PR job, I'll have to think about them too, but not for this case. I'd just like to have some verbal indication that Dougie was encouraged, spurred on to do what she did."

"I don't think we'll get it."

"Nor do I. Because I don't think it exists. I think that they were so close, so in each other's minds, that no word needed to be spoken. So even if she wanted to, Dougie could never honestly say she was doing what Jean wanted her to do. But I'm sure she *was*, all the same . . . Don't eat any more of that lamb if you don't want to."

"I do want to. I'm just interested in what we're talking about."

"I must learn some Indian dishes."

Eve didn't see the look of horror cast in her direction.

"Don't bother," said Rani. "You couldn't cook Indian better than an Indian, however hard you tried."

"I suppose your mother is a wonderful cook."

"She's a vile cook, but she's still better than you would be at Indian food. Stick to English and European— they're fine by me . . . Dougie was used to doing Jean's dirty work for her. She told us that herself."

"Oh yes. When she said that, I thought something was coming that could tie Jean in with the murder.

Instead it was the opposite. Sometimes Jean didn't even know that dirty work was being done for her by Dougie."

"Hmmm."

"Yes—what's the betting she had a pretty good idea? And with this relationship words didn't need to be spoken. A look of worry or apprehension, that gesture of dismissal when Evelyn Southwell's name came up, would be enough. Even if words were spoken, they didn't have to be direct. 'I just hope she'll keep quiet' doesn't count as encouragement, but it is very close to 'I just hope she'll be *kept* quiet.' The bond between them was so tight, so perverse—it was like Iago and Othello's. Othello does Iago's murder for him, and destroys himself utterly. Dougie does Jean's for her and goes to jail for years, and Jean speaks kindly of her, says it was an attack of madness."

"And goes her way. And what do you think will happen when Dougie comes out of jail?"

"Jean will be in another relationship, and there will be no room for Dougie."

"Mightn't that mean that Dougie will speak at last?"

"It could do, I suppose. Not that it will make any difference. You know more about this than I do, but no one, surely, would want to prosecute Jean on the say-so of a convict and former lover once she's got out of jail and found she's been thrown over."

"No, of course they wouldn't prosecute."

"She's got away with it, all right."

"And it pains you?"

"It pains like hell."

"You're becoming a sort of policeman already."

"*Not* a policeman," said Eve firmly. "I couldn't bear all the frustrations and disappointments when cases didn't get solved, or nobody got prosecuted for them . . . I keep going over in my mind the connections I had with Jean and Dougie. That time I phoned them, after I'd talked to Evelyn Southwell. They were both in Dougie's flat, because I phoned the number she gave me. Jean answered, and immediately twigged who I was and realized I needed to be handed on to Dougie, the 'Jean' I was used to. When she took the phone she thanked the fake 'Dougie.' It was all so smooth, so confident, so fraudulent."

"So rehearsed?" suggested Rani.

"You would have thought so. We were told Jean was angry with Dougie for pretending to be her, but she effortlessly fit in with the falsehoods."

"Jean had taken over Dougie, and she knew how to manipulate her. I bet your mother saw the danger because she was much more intelligent than Dougie."

"Oh, my mother! I think I begin to understand her. What a thing to say after all those years of being close to her! But there was so much I didn't know. She married very young—eighteen. I didn't realize that until I saw the marriage certificate. She never told me, and I bet that had to be concealed from the teachers' college. Then twelve years later I came along, probably meant to cement a failing marriage but for some reason not doing so. I suppose the likeliest reason was Jean. Though my mother was so much brighter than Dougie, she must have found Jean and her way of life a real temptation. Unless there's something I'm missing."

Later that evening, in the bed where May McNabb had

slept partnerless for all those years, Eve, happier than she had ever been in her life, said to Rani:

"Where do you want to get married?"

He looked at her quizzically.

"Where? Not when, by what rite, not in what building—the Crossley church, Windsor Castle, under the water in Lake Windermere, wherever?"

"Be serious, Omkar. You do want to get married, don't you?"

"More than you can imagine."

"Well then: England, India, Australia—where? Maybe somewhere where we have no friends and no baggage."

"India and Australia almost fit that bill. But why should we want a wedding with no friends? You've got practically no family, and mine will quite likely stay away. Looks like we may need friends."

"England, then. Britain, I should say. I have Scottish connections, though all the family ones are dead. You must manage to talk my father around to coming: assure him there is not the slightest danger of prosecution."

"I'll try. So it's Britain, probably Yorkshire, and either at a registry office or a church."

"Perhaps we could find a registry office with spiritual overtones. Or have a service of blessing, like Prince Charles. Or maybe the new laws mean we could make up our own marriage service and vows. I'm only the vaguest sort of Christian, and you're a pretty funny sort of Hindu."

They both giggled. But the next evening, when Rani was kept in Leeds working on the Southwell case and had phoned to say he would, with a bit of luck, be home by midnight, Eve decided she wanted to talk to her father.

"Dad?" she said, as soon as she could hear his voice. "It's early morning there, isn't it?"

"Yes. But I'm well up and my old machinery is oiled by two cups of tea and a couple of eggs, scrambled. It makes my day to hear from you."

"What's your news?"

"Not much. Oh well—something odd has happened, though it isn't going to shake the art world. Something has told me that my landscapes are never going to be much good, and I've switched to painting portraits."

"Not passersby in chalk on the pavement?"

"Cheeky child. Not at all. Australia is marvelous for faces, and Maconochie Harbour is full of sun-dried people with lizardlike faces and bodies, dried out but full of character and past exploits. I don't think I'm going to make a fortune, because people prefer to be flattered. This is a combination of my old cartoon skills and a switch to oils. I live in hope someone will commission me to paint the prime minister."

"They never will."

"No, they won't. Too scared of a demolition job, which I would be happy to provide. Whereas Kev the barman at the Ocean View thinks just getting a likeness is miraculously clever, is convinced that anything made by man knocks a mere photograph out of contention, and has absolutely no vanity. After a life of political cartooning it's a sort of liberation. So what's your news?"

"First—the murder of Evelyn Southwell. Jean Mannering's current lover and personal slave has been arrested. Jean is busy distancing herself, and the current betting is that the slave did it knowing full well this was what Jean wanted, but without any urging or conspiring. Hey presto—Jean is in the clear."

"What was the motive?"

"Evelyn was torturing them with the possibility of revelations about what happened thirty-odd years ago, when you were forced, persuaded, whatever, to leave the country and your wife and child."

"But what could she reveal?"

"Evelyn was at Heathrow, monitoring your departure."

There was a pause as he considered this.

"Well, that was an alliance made in hell. I hope my departure won't be something that is brought up at the trial."

"If she pleads guilty—as seems pretty certain she will— very little will come out at the trial."

"Good. And I presume the other news is your approaching marriage to Omkar?"

"It is. No great kudos in guessing that. We're planning it now."

"Did you consider having it in Australia?"

"We did. And having it in India. Both of them had the same drawback: we don't have any friends there."

"So you're staying in the old country," said her father, in a disconsolate voice. "I guessed you would in the end."

"Dad, there is no reason on earth why you shouldn't come back to the old country, as you call it. The police will probably be delighted that what Jean did back in the seventies fills in part of the picture of this present murder. There must be some part of you that wants to see the places that you knew again."

"It's a very, very small part."

"Only because you've got this idea you could be hauled in by the police or regarded as some kind of leper by old friends. As far as they're concerned, your marriage was breaking up, your health too, and you took off for Australia on a doctor's advice."

"And May told everyone I was dead."

"Okay—that was silly of her. I don't understand that. In fact, that's one of a thousand things I'd like to talk over with you—not on the phone, but with you here, beside me, chewing things over. I've got so many questions. Why did Mum not want you and me to have even a normal absentee parent and child relationship? Why was she happy in the relationship with Jean Mannering, when she had no history of lesbian interests? Why was your marriage falling apart when you'd at last had a child? Why had you married so early, I mean when May was so young? Why did you just give in when you were faced with Jean's demands? That's the oddest one to me. I don't see you as a quitter. You must have known your fingerprints couldn't have been on that pedophile pornography. Why did you go along with her demands so readily? Was it just because you and May were finished?"

There was silence at the other end. Then John McNabb, a crack in his voice, said:

"I think if I answer the last question, you'll be able to answer the others yourself. I may have held out hopes for our marriage, May's and mine, but at heart I knew it was over, and why. I didn't stand any chance of victory over Jean. You see, I knew that if the police were led to the porn in the Crossley house they'd want to look further, go to my other place of residence in Scotland. And when they went to my Glasgow flat, they'd have found more of the same. And it would have had my fingerprints on it."

Eve's heart sank and her eyes clouded with tears. She tried to say something, but nothing came. As she cleared her throat to try again, she heard the sound of the handset being replaced at the other end.

About the Author

ROBERT BARNARD's most recent novel is *A Fall from Grace.* Among his many other books are *The Graveyard Position, A Cry from the Dark, The Mistress of Alderley, The Bones in the Attic, A Murder in Mayfair, No Place of Safety, The Bad Samaritan* and *A Scandal in Belgravia.* Scribner released a classic edition of his *Death of a Mystery Writer* in 2002. He is the winner of the Malice Domestic Award for Lifetime Achievement and the prestigious Nero Wolfe Award, as well as the Anthony, Agatha and Macavity awards. An eight-time Edgar nominee, he is a member of Britain's distinguished Detection Club, and in May 2003, he received the Cartier Diamond Dagger Award for lifetime achievement in mystery writing. He lives with his wife, Louise, and their pets, Jingle and Durdles, in Leeds, England.